Under cover of night . . .

The sun would soon drop behind the mountain, plunging the little meadow into darkness. Foster would lose his advantage, and Muldoon would be able to see him better than he could be seen. It was a long shot for a pistol, and uphill. His first shot would have to count, or the Boy Stage Robber would be lobbing rifle slugs at them. Still, he was sitting up there smugly, dangling his legs like a child. Like shooting a bird off a tree branch. Muldoon felt much better now that he had a plan. He kept a close eye on the descending sun.

SETTLER'S LAW

D. H. Eraldi

BERKLEY BOOKS, NEW YORK

SETTLER'S LAW

A Berkley Book / published by arrangement with
the author

PRINTING HISTORY
Berkley edition / January 1999

The Penguin Putnam Inc. World Wide Web site address is
http://www.penguinputnam.com

ISBN: 0-425-16676-7

BERKLEY®
Berkley Books are published by The Berkley Publishing Group,
a member of Penguin Putnam Inc.,
375 Hudson Street, New York, New York 10014.
BERKLEY and the "B" design
are trademarks belonging to Berkley Publishing Corporation.

PRINTED IN THE UNITED STATES OF AMERICA

10 9 8 7 6 5 4 3 2 1

For Bonnie

and

for John

SETTLER'S LAW

PROLOGUE

Winter 1869

He expected to hang with Whitey and the others, but old Judge Carlyle just could not bring himself to condemn a thirteen-year-old boy. They made him watch, though. He'd seen the whole thing. He sat in the sod-walled storeroom used as a jail, and watched Whitey and Jed and the Tejano eat beans for their last supper.

The boy's plate sat untouched, the men's murmuring spilling around him unheard. At dawn he walked with them to the gallows steps, the silence so total that when Whitey turned to him and spoke it was like thunder from the flat clouds.

"You go home, Sett. Fix up that little cabin. Go back to your people. Tell 'em you're sorry." Then Whitey climbed up to end his life dangling against the brightening sky.

ONE

Spring 1883

He lay on his belly in the shadows of the pines and watched down on the homestead. The rocky ledge crumbled away to a grassy slope and then stretched mildly toward the cabin with its rail corral and feeble garden patch. There was a woman kneeling in the garden, her back to him as he squinted from his hiding place.

It was so familiar, even with the new barn where he remembered a shed. This was foolish, hiding up here when he wanted to jump up on the fine bay mare behind him and gallop into that spring-fed meadow with a whoop to announce his arrival, like when he was a kid rounding up the team for his father. But he was no kid now.

He squirmed forward on his elbows, pine needles working their way through his shirt and into the front of his pants. He did not flinch, intent on watching the woman in the garden. Was it her? A bonnet covered her head, and the voluminous skirts spread in the dark tilled soil, concealing her shape as she planted this year's vegetables. The sun had moved from one treetop to another. Still he waited.

The fine bay mare snorted softly from her picket. Sett scrambled backward from the edge and rolled over to check on her. She was a prize. Tall and elegant, out of place wearing his old beat-up saddle and the bedroll and saddlebags hanging off the side. Sett won her in a poker game, barely able to contain the surprise as he gazed down on a handful of spades and bet a month's wages. The foreman had placed the filly's papers on the table, and Sett laid down his cards. He asked for a bill of sale, and went out to the corral to see his new horse.

One look, and Sett was saddling up the rough colt he had ridden in on and tossing a catch loop over the sleek brown neck of the tall filly. In his hurry to get out of the little town, he paused at the mercantile and spent some of the winnings on a rifle and a long coat, then he disappeared into the back country and began the rambling journey north.

But the good horse did not make him any more welcome at the farms and towns he passed. More than once Sett had been accused of stealing the horse, mostly by men who learned his name. It bothered him, but he guessed it was to be expected. A man with his history riding a fine big horse, and traveling hard.

"Hooo, mare," Sett crooned to settle the horse below him in the trees. She gazed at him with huge dark eyes, mare-ish ears swiveled to catch the familiar voice. Sett wondered if she understood his thoughts, they were in such close company. The poker game had been a stroke of great luck, he reflected, and he did not consider himself particularly lucky. In fact his life seemed much the opposite. Winning big was perhaps a good sign. He considered this as he crawled back to his lookout over the homestead. Even with the newer barn, it was modest. The log house, bare front and single window, looked as he remembered it. The garden was in the same plot between the barn with its abundant manure supply and the spring. One hundred sixty acres, not really enough to ranch and not the country to farm. Still, it was his family's, or had been. A lot of thought went into coming back here, fourteen years' worth of thought. Now he hid above his home and watched a woman in the garden.

The door to the cabin swung open and a figure stepped out. Female, obviously, and young. Sett calculated the years. He studied her as she walked across the worn grass yard to the spring and bent to fill a bucket. As if resigned, her shoulders drooped and her head bobbed with every step. Sett strained to catch a glimpse of her face as she trudged to join the other woman in the tilled earth.

Elizabeth had looked like him, and like younger brother Ben, all three with their mother's deep hazel eyes and square jaw, all three with their father's golden hair and tall build. But Elizabeth had been hardly more than a toddler when he had last seen her.

Neither woman looked up. They seemed oblivious to the mountains behind them, unaware of the red fox sneaking along the meadow behind the cabin, and clearly unconcerned that someone could be watching.

Sett could never remember being that unwary in the yard. Things must be more civilized around here nowadays, but there must still be the occasional Indian and horse thief, along with the more common dangers of chicken-thief coyotes and bears.

He pushed back from the rock and uncoiled himself to full height. Brushing dust off, he unbuttoned his trou-

sers to shake out the needles. He tried to wipe off the
grime and stains from his trip, finally going to the roll
on his saddle and extracting a clean version of the Henley shirt he wore. The better shirt in one hand, Sett
rubbed his face with the other. When had he last shaved?
Two, three days? Maybe he should look for a spot downstream to bathe. Hell, he wasn't going courting. Maybe
they wouldn't even speak to him. Maybe they had forgotten.

But he knew that wasn't true. He'd gotten two letters
when he was still in prison. His family knew he was
there and so they must know what he'd done. He hadn't
written back. He had used the two separate sheets of
paper to roll cigarettes with tobacco smuggled in by his
cell mate. He sat very quiet when he smoked the scrap
on which his father had scrawled, ''Ben died last night
of the cholera. Your mother is well.'' Sett thought on
that a long time. His mother was well. As well as could
be with her eldest in prison and her other son newly
dead. But the second letter was worse, and written in a
strange feminine hand:

> We wanted you to know that Father died last week.
> Mother could not bring herself to write. He died
> quietly considering. We have hired a man to help
> with the ranch. Mother wants to stay. She speaks
> of you often and prays for you.
>
>> Your sister,
> > Elizabeth

So his mother was waiting for him. Had she any idea
how long a wait that would be? He carefully tore the
letter into little squares to share with Pablo. Four more
years. Four more years of sneaking smokes and listening

for the guard. Four more years of thin gruel and cold stone walls leaching moisture in the winter. Four lifetime years.

Sett yanked the shirt over his head so suddenly that the mare snorted and backed away. He grabbed up his hat from its resting place in the branches of a choke-cherry and waved it up to his head. When stepping over to the startled mare, though, he automatically slowed and quieted. "Hooo, mare," he breathed as he girthed her up and swung up onto her high back. At least he was arriving home on a good horse.

The mare walked light as a deer through the pine forest and down the slope. Sett was not consciously quiet, but when he rode out of the forest's darkness into the sunlight by the spring, the women in the garden still had not looked up. They were absorbed in dropping three tiny beans into each mound and carefully pouring water from the bucket into the trench. Sett slowed the horse even more, letting her snatch a bite of the meadow grass. Something was not right. His eyes wandered to the barn.

The buckboard was gone. He could see where it was usually parked by the shorter brown grass. No team in the corral. The man must be gone. He couldn't imagine riding right into the yard unnoticed if a man were there.

Sett scanned the yard without turning his head. He'd been wrong before. The cabin was changed. There was a lean-to room added on behind. As Sett watched, the door was slowly pulled closed. He heard the click of a droplatch in the still mountain air. No one recognized him. He'd have to introduce himself, if he were not shot first.

He let the mare drift to a stop behind the women. They were talking in hushed tones, conspiring. Sett licked his dry lips and tried to summon his voice.

The horse did it for him. Her snort caused the women to stiffen, and the younger one turned to gaze at him. She parted her full mouth but held the scream. Sett never took his eyes off the kneeling figure before him.

"Mama?" His voice was a whisper. The woman turned, and Sett stared into the round blue eyes and heavy-boned face of a stranger.

Ria knew he was coming before he'd cleared the forest. Ravens flew up from the nesting trees and the young cow elk who slept in the grove sauntered out—here, at midday. Something was coming down the hill, not a very threatening something, but not a familiar something either. She left off gathering kindling, called her dog to her and began to slide quietly back to the cabin, keeping it between herself and the hay meadow. She could not see Ma'am and Carolyn working in the garden on the other side. Probably nattering away on their plans to escape this homestead in the wilds, when it was she who should be seeking escape.

The stocky blue dog trailed right at her feet, practically stepping into the folded grass of her soft footprints. The dog paused, and raised her pointy muzzle to sample the air. The low growl was hushed by a look. They both heard slow hoofbeats, almost wandering through the grass. A riderless horse? Ria moved again, crouching in the tall growth along the back of the lean-to. Careful to keep one hand on Coy, she peered around the corner.

A man. A strange man on a fine horse.

There were no sounds in the house, no hello from the garden, no surprised greeting. Only a silent man riding into the yard, and Ma'am and Carolyn preoccupied with counting seed beans.

The door into the lean-to opened just off the side, but

the man appeared to be concentrating on the women in the garden. She slipped in now before he got any closer.

Dumb white women. She brushed under the blanket hanging over the doorway and carefully pulled the rifle from the corner by the sewing cabinet. *Dumb as sheep. Come all the way out here dragging a china cupboard.* Still, she would catch hell if they lived through whatever this became and found a ding in the prize furniture. She glanced over at the dog, lying ears pricked and worried. Then she looked out the window.

The man must have said something. Both women had turned and Carolyn was staring at him with the beginning of panic on her face. The man sat motionless, tightness in his shoulders. Ria put the gun up on the windowsill, and waited.

Carolyn's face was turning pale, and Ria had the fleeting memory of her fainting when Augie had killed the hog. Ria had never seen anyone faint like that, white hankie raised to cover her face as the pale skin turned even whiter and the trembling knees folded. Ria had laughed, straightening up from the butchering with hog blood on her hands and the skinning knife, but Ma'am and Augie had rushed to Carolyn's side. The laughter had earned her a beating. Now she did not smile at Carolyn's paleness.

This dirty blond man on the obviously stolen horse, he looked like he could rob someone. Maybe kill them. But the rifle was in the scabbard and the hands folded on the saddle horn. He took a deep breath, squared his shoulders and shook his head as if stunned.

Suddenly he leaned over the mare's neck.

"Where are they? Where are the people who used to be here?"

The intensity of the movement drew Ria's eye. The

rifle muzzle that had been hovering in the man's general direction now locked on to him as she sighted. It would be good if he scared the dumb women away, but she would not let him harm them. Augie would not like that. She held her bead just under the buttons of the Henley, but the man did not reach for the rifle or move toward his belt. His eyes scanned the yard, across the tilled earth of the garden, past the outhouse by the edge of the forest, and stopped on the cabin window with the muzzle resting on the sill.

Finally, a use for the curtains Ma'am had insisted on hanging over the window hole in the log wall.

Ria held her breath. The man looked back at the women. He sat very quiet for a long time, the only sound being Carolyn's attempts to control her sobs. Ria held him in the rifle sights. He was no fool. He knew she was there.

She admired his control, how slowly he shifted his weight to the left and swung his leg over the broad rump of the horse, how he touched the ground as if a bird were landing, how he turned his back directly to her as he entered the dark plot of the garden. He reached up and removed the soiled hat.

"I'm sorry to frighten you, ma'am," he said as he took the woman's arm to help her up, "but this is my home."

Sett wondered when the person in the cabin would make an appearance. He expected shouts, or bullets, but not a sound came from the rifleman with the advantage. The woman was brushing off her skirt with fingers spread and the younger one was finally catching her breath between little chokes. There was sure enough to ask, but under rifle sights, it seemed best to play polite.

"What do you mean, this is your home?" Constance Johnson drew herself up to her shoulders-back stance. Her voice pinched out her nose and Sett could recognize nothing of his mother in her. Where was her man, in the cabin? She did not even glance toward it.

"I mean, I grew up here. This is my family's homestead." Sett kept his back to the gunman. At least this wasn't a hasty man with the trigger. The longer they stood here without shots, the better, Sett figured. He wasn't the type to shoot someone in the back.

"I didn't mean to frighten you. I just wanted to surprise my . . . people. I thought you were them." Sett swung a low-headed glance toward the cabin. "Do you know anything about them? Name's Foster. I'm Sett Foster." The woman did not appear to recognize his name. Maybe the reputation had not gotten here faster than he had.

"I never heard of your people. Of course, Carolyn and I are new here, so we are not well versed in the history. My husband could tell you more. He took this place four years ago. It was abandoned."

"Is your husband here?" Sett tried to smile, or at least look unthreatening.

"Pa went to Verdy. He'll be back any minute!" The daughter looked pointedly down the wagon tracks. Her mother clenched her already tight jaw.

"Carolyn, hush," she commanded.

"He'll be back any minute now," the girl repeated, "any minute."

Dithering little piece, Sett thought.

"So who's holding the rifle on me from the cabin?" Sett asked quietly. He turned and stared right at the single window.

•　　•　　•

Ria froze as the stranger turned to look at her. She
only hear snatches of what was said, but she didn't ̇ ̇s
Carolyn's fluttering hands or Ma'am's stiff back. Carolyn's eyes followed the man's gaze to the window.

"Mama, it's the Injun girl," she whispered. The man
glanced at her.

Ria took new grip on the rifle stock and again held
bead on the space below his third shirt button. He took
her for scared. Now he knew she was a woman and he
took her for scared! If he was threatening, if he touched
Ma'am or Carolyn . . . but he just watched the window,
even though he could not possibly see more than a
shadow, his dark eyes seeking her out. Ria focused on
the spot on his chest and tried to avoid his eyes. She
was not a swooner, not like Carolyn, who had just betrayed her.

Damn them, damn these two women who had dropped
into her life against her will. It would be easier to let
this smooth thief have them, to kill them or whatever it
was he wanted, and use the diversion to be on her way.
She could head north, to the land of her grandfather. Her
mother was the daughter of a medicine chief, it was said.
But where were these people, and how to get to them?
She had no idea. This cabin was her home now, and
these women were no happier here than she, of this she
was sure. They were only here because of Augie; Mr.
Johnson she was supposed to call him since his white
wife and daughter had come west. Silly women, so busy
counting beans and hatching plans instead of listening
and watching that a stranger had ridden up behind them.
But she could not abandon them now. She would not.

Ria dropped her shoulder to ease the building ache.
The man still faced her in the garden, his long coat
pulled back around his hands on his hips. There were

no pistols. His rifle was in the saddle scabbard on the
bay mare cropping grass outside the garden fence. She
let herself look at his face, the deep-eyed face that
needed a shave. What was it he'd said when he rode up
behind the women in the garden? Mama?

The cabin door swung open. Sett showed no surprise,
no motion to express his reaction to the small dark figure. She was not much more than a girl, dressed in a
odd mixture of blue calico and beaded leather. It had
been a long time since he had seen a native woman in
leggins, but the memory was vivid: Old Talking Crow,
his sons with their families behind him, standing in this
very yard. Sett's father, joking and strong and meeting
their eyes. Moses Foster had been the earliest of the
settlers, and friend of all the neighbors on the plain, including the Blackfeet.

Talking Crow's women dressed like this, but this girl
was not all Indian. Her long braids were dark brown,
not black, and her skin was almost creamy. Her eyes,
though, were the color of chocolate. Startling as her appearance was to him, it was the dog at her side that held
the man's attention. As Sett started toward them, the
merle dog rose and braced her front legs. The bitch's
lips curled a bit and an inaudible growl tipped her head.
The girl's eyes showed no fear. The rifle was carried in
the crook of her arm, ready. The dog told him when to
stop, and he was closer than he expected to be, all given.
He tried to smile, sorry again that he had skipped the
bath. Sett suddenly missed his father. What would he do
with this fierce little woman defending her home?

"I'm sorry to have startled you," he began.

"No, not startled." She looked him in the eyes. So
calm and different than the two blond women in the

garden, she seemed totally in control of herself, her dog and even of him. "We know you were coming before they did." She nodded her head toward the nervous women.

"Your dog didn't bark."

"She does not bark, except in play."

"And you?" Sett shifted his weight and rested his hand on his hip. It drew her eyes to the knife sheath on his belt. Suddenly she felt that he was quite well armed, even with his rifle in the saddle scabbard forty feet away.

"What do you want? You snuck in here quiet." Now it was his turn to notice a shift in grip on the long rifle. She asked a good question. What was he doing here? Sett paused and checked back on the two women in the vegetable garden. The young one was casting quick looks down the wagon tracks, the older one watching him with a curious face. "And why call her Mama? You don't look like her son."

"I'm not. I was raised here, this is my family's homestead." Sett shook his head. "At least it was. I've been gone a long time. I wanted to surprise my family."

"Not sure of your welcome?" She tilted her head back to squint at him.

"No, not quite." Growing up in prison had not prepared him for this. She reminded him of the badger in the hay meadow, protective, dangerous. And attractive. As a boy he had lain in the grass and watched the sow around her burrow, admiring her pelt and scheming to trap her the next winter. But that next winter had found him in the Tenderfoot holding Whitey's horses while Whitey shot the stage driver. The last time he was here, there was a badger in the hay meadow; now there was a badger in the doorway of his home.

Sett finally smiled. After all the months of traveling, all the nights of worry and speculation, after the shock of the strange-faced woman in the garden—here was someone familiar.

TWO

The barroom of the Silver Slipper glowed with an amber light, and August Johnson smiled with satisfaction just to be standing in the doorway. It had been nearly a year since he had last visited civilization, excepting when he had come in to pick up Connie and Carolyn, and then a journey to the Silver Slipper had been out of the question. He surveyed the room. His barn was bigger. The saloon was squeezed into a narrow two-story building between the livery and the hotel, each appearing to hold the other up in the brisk winds that swept across the pass. Mining towns grew where the ore was, and this one had had the great luck of being on the stage line and, later, a stop on the railroad, giving it a life beyond the boom of '63. Augie scratched absentmindedly under his ribs as he looked for red-haired Maggie. It would be a disappointment if she had moved on, but the bar appeared well stocked and a thin man with a handlebar mustache was watching him intently from behind it. Augie stepped into the golden light and rested his elbows at the near end of the bar.

"Whiskey," he ordered and the thin fellow quickly complied. Augie downed the whiskey, then turned to continue the search for Maggie. Ah, there was the cascading red hair, way in the back at the card table. She was perched next to a hatted man, overlooking his hand with her back to Augie. August Johnson was in no hurry. He was here for the night, and he intended to get the most out of his brief time in town.

By leaving the homestead at sunup and driving the empty wagon steadily all day, he had reached Verdy just before dark. The mules were cranky, but at least he was not camping out on the prairie. With the mules and their nasty tempers in the livery corral, he could be sure of getting his money's worth of the communal feed. He'd load the wagon tomorrow morning and leave by midday, still arriving home in three days and having a night to enjoy the delights of Verdy, Montana.

Augie's idea of delights had been few and far between these past years. The owlhoot trail he'd traveled had not led to the promised good life in the frontier. It was a wild country out here, and at first the idea that he would not see a single soul, white or Injun or nigger, for months at a time had bothered him a great deal. Still, he had to stay and look. It was his best chance to strike it rich.

It was the loneliness of the place that had prompted him to buy the breed girl, and to send a message to his abandoned wife in Kentucky, but right at the moment he could not think of a better cure for the Montana homestead blues than another shot of whiskey and a turn at Maggie of the Silver Slipper.

Augie crooked a beefy finger at the barkeep, who came scuttling up with the bottle.

"I'll take this with me," he said as his hand enveloped the neck of the bottle and he made his way to an empty table where he could catch Maggie's eye.

Maggie avoided his gaze. She had seen him in the doorway, recognizing him from the year before as the filthy mule skinner he was, even though he claimed to have a ranch in the Cottonwood Mountains. She studiously watched the card game going on in front of her. This Muldoon she was courting had at least bathed and shaved upon his arrival in town, and was betting like his money belt was heavy. Maggie snuggled a little closer to the man in the black hat, letting her breast graze his hand as he held the cards up for her inspection. Looked like he would have more coins to share in a few moments.

Augie watched the card players lay down their hands, shake their heads and frown as the winner swept the pot into his corner.

"Ah, Muldoon, I shoulda knowed better than to sit to poker with you," one of them complained as he rose from the chair. Muldoon flashed what passed for a smile on his gray face, the skin around his mouth twitching and the eyebrows cocking upward.

Augie froze with his glass raised halfway to his lips. He stared at the man. It couldn't be, he thought, but it was. Hardly recognizable in the clean white shirt and black dandy vest, derby tapped down on the brownish hair, Captain R. J. Muldoon, formerly of the Bluegrass Rebels, and more recently the object of an arrest warrant for robbery, conspiracy and murder. Augie was shocked to meet him here, here of all places. Somehow Muldoon had escaped the vigilantes. Of course Augie himself had survived, so why should he be surprised that his old captain, a far more clever man than himself, could still be roaming around after that wild raiding. What was it, four, five years ago?

Augie brought the glass the rest of the way to his mouth and swallowed. So here was Cap'n Muldoon, his old partner on the owlhoot, the reason Augie was in this godforsaken wilderness in the first place, and sitting with red-haired Maggie, no less. Augie poured one more drink from the bottle, downed it and rose before it could take effect. He stepped over to the card table and stood with long arms hanging down, saying nothing until Muldoon finally looked up at him.

"Evening, Cap'n, Maggie." Augie nodded to each.

Muldoon peered up at the burly man. He could smell him even in this shit-hole bar, a sour smell of fresh mule sweat and stale human. He leaned back to reveal the handle of the revolver. The man in front of him was not surprised. Muldoon squinted at the bland face: a little close between the eyes, straight nose, homemade haircut.

Maggie edged away. She did not like Augie Johnson, found him to be more work than the coin was worth. Muldoon might take care of him for her.

But Muldoon made no move for a long time, then he motioned to the empty chair.

"Johnson. Sit down." He turned to Maggie. "Bring us another bottle, dear, would you?" As Maggie went to the bar, Augie sat heavily in the chair opposite Muldoon.

"Fancy seeing you here. What brings you to Verdy?" Muldoon took out a tobacco pouch and began to roll a cigarette. Augie watched the slender fingers manipulate the fine paper. Muldoon always took care of his hands; there were no calluses or small injuries.

"Came in for supplies, Cap'n. I got me a homestead over in the Cottonwood Mountains." Augie waited for a reaction, pouring himself another drink from the new bottle.

"The Cottonwoods, you say." Muldoon tipped his head as if appreciating the news. "No need to call me Captain; I am just a private businessman now." He lit the cigarette and slid the makings across the table to Augie. "Just where abouts is your farm?"

"On Cairn Creek, the old Foster place. It's a ranch. I got sheep."

"No offense, now, Johnson. I suppose you are also doing some, shall we call it, prospecting? Any luck?"

Augie glared at the man across from him. Muldoon was twirling his glass slowly in one hand, never sloshing the liquid, seldom taking a sip. This Muldoon, what an aggravating asshole he was. Augie had been assigned to Muldoon's personal staff, a job that consisted mostly of pitching the captain's tent and packing his personal effects. He had to admire the man though. When it came to the business of killing, and preserving his hide at the same time, there was none better than R. J. Muldoon. Too bad his postwar plan for big riches had not worked out. Augie would already be living the good life in California, instead of searching the Foster homestead. Ah, but without Muldoon, Augie would not even have known to look. He finished his whiskey and Muldoon quickly poured him another glass.

"No luck, no luck yet." Augie leaned closer. "Them mountains are a big place." Augie tried to sort out where Maggie was hiding. The flickering lights were swimming and he did not want to miss out on his civilized entertainment by passing out first.

Muldoon watched him reel a little in his chair. "Well, Johnson, it was clever of you to think of homesteading that place. Not a bad little ranch. How long you been

out there?'' Muldoon noticed the drunk man perk up at
the praise.

'' 'Bout three, four years. I circled back after we split
up. I'm all respectable now, brought my wife and daughter out.'' Augie tried to smile but it faded down to a
grimace. ''Honestly, Cap'n, I'd like to finish with this
prospectin' and get on to somewhere warm. I'd just like
to know where it was. Don't think you could help me,
do ya? For an old pard?''

Muldoon smiled to himself. Same old Johnson, strong
in the body and weak between the ears. Same old gul-
lible, drunk Johnson. He beckoned to Maggie at the bar.

''One thing, old friend, before I sign on to help you
with this treasure hunt, has the boy shown up?''

''The boy?'' Augie echoed blearily.

''Yes, the Foster boy. You know, the boy stage robber, the one with Whitey Kennady?''

Augie shook his head. ''Ain't seen no boy. Ain't seen
nobody. It's lonely as hell out there. Why, had to go buy
me a squaw . . .''

Muldoon interrupted to address Maggie. ''Take my
old partner here upstairs. Seems he's been lonely
lately.'' Maggie started to refuse. Augie Johnson was
now not only dirty, but very drunk. She looked Muldoon
in the eyes, saw what was there, and helped Augie out
of the chair.

Ria walked through the late afternoon sunshine, making
her way along the splashing edges of the trace where
the spring ran down to meet the main creek. She carried
a dinner pail of leftover beans and biscuits, a reason for
traipsing down the canyon. She followed a fishing trail,
and made unconscious note of the dark shadows of the

trout in the dappled pools, but she was not thinking about fishing right now.

The stranger said he would camp down at the old summer grounds, the hunting camp in the crook of the stream above the beaver ponds. She knew the place. She should not have been surprised. He had lived here longer than she had.

Once her defensiveness had dropped, she had found herself standing shyly on the porch step while Ma'am and Carolyn inched closer to hear what the tall man said. Not that they could answer his questions. They knew nothing about the clearing with its large fire ring and tent frames. They were just glad when he left the yard, even though Carolyn's insistence that Augie would be back soon only meant that the man on the big horse would return the next day.

Ria skipped across the stones of the crossing, her dog wading through the water and pausing to lap up a drink. Ria waited for her, impatient to continue down to the clearing. She wanted to look at the man again, to decide if he could be trusted enough to talk to, to ask questions.

Then she had to really think. How to word the questions? She seldom said anything to Augie, and she had worked to understand his few terse orders. Talking in the white man's tongue was difficult, not like talking to LaBlanc in the lodge along the Missouri.

Sett Foster had called it the old Blackfeet camp, and she wondered if he knew the people who had camped there. Her curiosity drew her down the canyon, that chance that the stranger would know where her mother's people were, that he could tell her. She thought again about asking the question, and the stranger's own words echoed in her head. *Where are they? Where are the people who used to be here?*

Sett Foster had offered no explanations as to why he did not know where his family was, but Ria knew. She had been on Foster Creek long enough to hear the stories. Ma'am and Carolyn should know them, too, but they seldom took the time to listen, so intent on returning to civilization were they. Ria had lived in this cabin for three years. She knew things about the Foster homestead, some that Sett Foster didn't.

He should know, although she could not decide why she owed him this.

From through the aspens she could hear splashes and whooshes and shouts, not like a battle, but more of a playful sound. Ria stepped cautiously to the edge of the clearing. The outlaw Sett Foster was taking a bath.

He stood in the center of the beaver pond, its mountain waters swirling around his thighs. He was truly tall, she realized. She watched him scrub sand into the rag-mop light hair and bend over to submerge his head to rinse it out. Ria choked down a laugh. He did not look so dangerous now with his head under water and his white ass in the air. His clothes were on the bank, drying in the sun. Quite a tidy stagecoach robber he was.

She had begun to wonder if he were trying to drown himself when he stood up and gasped for breath. Coy began to growl and from the picket in the shade the big horse pricked her ears and snorted. Sett finished shaking the water out of his eyes and looked up at her in the trees.

"I thought you would come later," he said wryly. He reached up to strip the water from his hair. An outdoorsmen, his face and arms were tanned deep brown, the rest of his lean body pale. Ria gazed with open curiosity. Naked children were no rarity, but she had seen few naked men.

Augie managed to live most his life without removing his baggy union suit. He always pointed out to her its conveniently placed flaps and buttons. Not at all the same as this thoroughbred man bathing in the stream. She stared solemnly as he waded toward her. He used his hands to strip the clinging water before taking the nearly dry breeches from the willows. He pulled them on, hopping on one foot then the other to do it. He sat in the grass and tied on his moccasins. They were not well made, she noted. She could do better. His boots with the jingly spurs were sitting neatly by the saddlebags. Sett finally stood and placed his worn hat on his wet head and turned to face her.

"Now that I am in shape to have visitors, come on in." He gestured toward the fire pit and pole shelter. There was a frying pan and a battered coffee tin next to the fire. A cleaned string of trout waited in the ripples of the creek. Ria remembered the pail of biscuits and beans she was holding. It seemed a poor excuse now, but she walked down the bank into the camp with Coy at her side.

She held out the pail. Sett started to reach for it but the little dog bared her teeth and looked up at him with half-closed eyes.

"Better set it over there." He leaned back and reached for his belt and knife hanging in the trees. The girl was still armed. "You get a lot of practice sneaking up on people."

"So do you." Ria put the dinner pail down and turned to face him. She stared at him silently, watching him buckle on the belt. Clean, his hair was a warm gold, and his face looked younger, even with its growth of stubble. It was a nice face, a face that could smile. She tried to choose some words.

"This camp. The people that were here?"

She spoke with a soft accent, the words rolling familiar in a voice too deep for her years. Sett narrowed his eyes. "What about them?"

"They were Blackfeet?"

"The people who made this camp? Yes." Now he was curious. It was not the line of questioning he had expected.

"Maybe they were my people. Where are they?"

"It was a long time ago. The last time I saw them, they were heading north, over the pass. Maybe on the reservation. Maybe in Canada." The girl's face fell, disappointment darkening the fine features. Sett waited.

"I know who you are," she said suddenly.

"Really?"

"Did you escape from jail?"

"No, my time was up." Sett settled against the log placed as a seat for the fire.

"Did you steal that horse?" She tipped her dark head toward the mare.

"Nope, won her in a poker game." The breed girl widened her eyes skeptically. "A fair game, too, just my lucky night."

Sett examined the contents of the pail. "These biscuits any good?"

"I made them. Why did you come back here?"

"I didn't ask if you made 'em, I asked if they're good." Sett brought his eyes up to meet hers and she saw the spark of anger. His body was relaxed, legs folded, shoulders level, but that was deceiving.

As if reading her thoughts, he reached to the back of his belt and extracted a short knife from the sheath. He sliced one of the biscuits in half. "I've answered all your questions honestly. Why don't you do the same for me?

Sit down. Help yourself.'' Sett motioned at the log. Ria sat at the end and Coy lay at her feet. "I came here to find my family, as I said before.'' Sett talked around a mouthful of biscuit. "You think you know who I am? Who exactly am I? I don't even know. If you know all so much, why don't you fill me in?''

Ria drew a deep breath. She wished she had not come here to his camp. The sun was low over the hills and frogs were beginning to sing from the marshy banks. She wanted to leave. How quickly the tall outlaw with his polite ways had gone from naked silliness in the beaver pond to unnerving presence. She would have to be more careful.

"I must go. Ma'am will look for me." Ria started to get up. Sett motioned back to the log with the knife.

"Sit," he said as if he were talking to the dog. "Why did you come down here? It wasn't to bring me these dry old biscuits. I traveled a long way to get here, only to find my family gone and my house full of frilly city women and an uppity half-breed. I answered your questions. You answer mine. You said you knew who I was, so who am I?''

"You robbed the stage," she finally blurted, "you killed that man.''

"Does everyone think that?''

Ria's cheeks reddened. She nodded.

He rose to his feet, and paced a slow circle around the firepit, one palm rubbing his jaw. He had still not shaved, his plans having been disrupted by this tiny girl. He could get better information out of his horse.

Sett watched her as he paced. Her dark eyes followed him back and forth, quiet and without fear. There was something there, a familiarity of expression that sat comfortably in his memory. As she perched cross-legged on the log, her hands folded into her lap, he thought he saw someone else.

"I wasn't there when Whitey shot that driver. I heard the shots, but I was up the canyon holding the horses." Now Sett paused in front of her, towering over her. "Now, answer my question. Where are my people?"

Ria looked away. She had come here to tell him this, but how to say it? The silence stretched too long. Sett Foster leaned down to stare into her eyes, and the sudden movement brought Coy onto her feet with a growl. Ria opened her mouth, wishing words would form without her conscious effort. "There are graves on the hillside."

"I know that." The man stepped back, wary.

"There are five graves." She held up her small hand, fingers spread.

Sett did not move for many breaths, then he turned and resumed his circuit around the fire.

Ria watched as the man made another pass in front of her, the toe of his moccasin rubbing a dimple in the earth as he pivoted and turned in the same spot. She waited for him to say something, to stop and recognize her, but as the sun disappeared behind the pines on the ridge, she shifted uncomfortably. He did not appear to notice; his footfalls were as rhythmic as time ticking. Finally she stood, and when he did not even glance her way, she slipped out of the camp, the dog following quietly at her heels.

She broke into a run as soon as she reached the trees, the sound startling Sett out of his reverie. Dusk surrounded him, the fire had sputtered to coals, and the mare was watching him, waiting patiently for her dinner. He went over to the saddlebags and pulled out a sack of oats. It was nearly empty, and he poured it all on the ground for the mare. As she chewed contentedly, Sett rested his back against the smooth bark of an aspen and rolled around in his mind what the girl had told him.

Five graves, two of course his father's and brother's. Three more. Sett leaned his head on his arms and swallowed against the thickness in his throat. His mother and his sister dead? Some unknown hired man too. Darkness advanced through the aspen grove and the creek bubbled cheerily. From here in the trees, Sett could see his camp in the clearing, the same clearing where he had peered at Whitey and Jed and the Tejano on a night as calm as this one nearly fifteen years ago. A long time, now forever. The years in the cold cell, the days of hard riding and nights of speculation and practiced apologies, the loneliness that he had chosen while waiting to return somehow to that previous life, all were dashed away. There were strangers in his house. There were five graves on the pretty wildflowered knoll.

Carolyn was sitting on Ria's bed examining Ria's latest beading project. She hardly moved when Ria slid panting through the door.

"You were gone a long time," she said mildly. "Did it go well with Mr. Foster?"

"We talked." Ria took the leather garment from her hands and folded it into the sewing basket.

"Oh, I'm sure you found out all about the man who says he lived here. Does he want the ranch?" Carolyn paused to check on the snores issuing from her mother's pallet in the main room. "Mother says he does. Mother says maybe Papa will try to fight him. She says it was a lie that he's looking for his family."

"No lie, his family is in the graveyard."

"What graveyard?" Carolyn hardly ever ventured beyond the garden plot and the outhouse.

Ria shook her head and tried to wave the blond girl off her bed.

Carolyn ignored her. "Does he know you come with the house?"

Ria's face flushed and she spoke through gritted teeth. "Go. Go."

Carolyn stood slowly and gave a little half bow. "Maybe that's why you went out to his camp. To tell him." She ducked beneath the blanket that covered the doorway into the main cabin.

Ria pulled off her moccasins and her dress. She burrowed under the blankets as Coy jumped onto the foot of the bed. But she lay with her brown eyes wide open. She came with the house. That was how Augie had explained her to his newly arrived wife and daughter. They thought she was a servant, a slave, and Augie would not correct them.

Ria remembered that day too clearly. Augie had told her he was going to the train to collect the wife from Kentucky. He had explained that the new wife was called Ma'am, and his name would be Sir from now on. Ria had accepted that, as she did all of Augie's orders. While he was gone, she cleaned and cooked, wanting to be a good example for the new wife, and wanting to be clear that her house was well managed.

A second wife could be a great help. Her own mother had been the second wife of the trapper LaBlanc, and Ria was ready to welcome the company of another woman to the wilderness homestead. On the day Augie was to return, she dressed in her best leggins and poncho. She had burned sweetgrass in the cabin and wrapped her braids with otter fur. When she heard the wagon approaching, she waited inside the cabin, as first wife should. But Augie had shouted for her to come out and unload the wagon. Ma'am had sailed in the door and stopped stock-still at the sight of her.

"What is this!" the large pale woman had demanded, pointing a finger at Ria. Then Augie had explained that this was Ria and she, uh, came with the house. Ria had carried load after load of boxes from the wagon and helped Augie carry the glass-fronted china cupboard into the cabin. She could feel her face burning to this day.

Neither of these white women understood that this was her house, that she had been the only wife here for three years. Ria was more than prepared to share Augie, but she could not give up her authority as first wife. She was so alone. Augie sided with Ma'am and Carolyn, changing the rules as he saw fit. For all these years Ria had lived at this homestead, run the house, prepared for winter, gathered and hunted and moved with the rhythms of the mountains, and now a woman from some place called Kentucky, a woman who was so unaware that she let a stranger ride into the yard without knowing he was coming, this woman gave her orders and she was supposed to obey. Ria lay in the blackness of the lean-to room and cried without making a sound.

THREE

Sett shook off his blankets at first dawn and mounted the bay mare bareback. He had never been to the family cemetery, but he knew right where it would be. From the camp downstream he wound his way through the small pines and chokecherries. He passed the barnyard. Again the blue bitch did not bark. He decided that Ria must be up, but no sign of life issued from the cabin.

The mare waded knee-deep in the rich spring grass, dew from the night chill wetting her long legs. Above the log buildings the canyon opened out into the hay meadow, its spring-irrigated crop studded with blue wild irises. As the sun filtered over the mountains, Sett turned up a worn trail through the boulders. The path had not been used regularly, as it had when he was a boy. Still, he knew every twist in its course: the grassy elk park under the aspens and the spot where his mother had surprised a bear on her Sunday journey to the church clearing. She had thumped her palm on the leather cover of the Bible, making a loud enough *swack*! to send the bear lumbering off into the trees and to bring her husband running up the trail behind her.

Rose Foster had been undaunted, sure that the good Lord would not allow her to be eaten by a bear on her way to church. She continued her Sabbath practice, conceding only to Moses carrying a rifle as they climbed each Sunday up the sheltering ridge and out to the clearing.

There was no building, but nature made up for that with a sweeping view of the valley and high plains that stretched west to kiss the horizon.

"No better temple than this God-given earth," Rose was fond of exclaiming as her husband and young sons knelt beside her in prayer, later joined by baby Elizabeth wrapped in a trade blanket. Sett remembered staring off into the distance, lost in daydreams of what lay on the other side of the valley, the other side of the Rocky Mountains, the other side of the world. He remembered being startled when the rest of the family had broken into "Old One Hundred" while he was imagining riding into the wilderness beside Talking Crow and his people. He remembered his voice cracking between its childhood soprano and deep tenor, his mother ignoring the mutilation of the hymn, and his father winking at him proudly.

The fine mare broke the clearing, and Sett slid down and looped her reins over a tree branch. The view was much the same, expanse beyond comprehension, only now there were five weathered headboards sitting silently where his family used to kneel.

Sett skirted the clearing until he was in front of the lonely monument. Farthest left was his younger brother, the name Foster carved deeply in the top of the board and the legend *Beloved Brother Benjamin 1856–71*. The next marker was similarly carved for Moses, *Beloved Father*. The last three were plainer, quicker, saying simply *Rose, Elizabeth* and, a little ways away, *Edward*. No dates, no clues.

Sett removed his hat and waited there in the light of a mountain morning. He tried to recall a prayer, but the only preaching that came to mind was the sad-eyed padre asking forgiveness over the bodies of Whitey, Jed and the Tejano before a photographer flashed their picture.

Sett slammed the hat back on his head, and turned to look out over the valley. His family had come a long way to lie here. He could barely remember the trip west. Such a lonely place to seek out with a wife and small children. Sett sank to the ground. Who was responsible for the deaths of his mother and sister? Was it this wild place, far from a doctor, and far from the help of a neighbor? This place with roaming renegades, bear and range fires? The anger at not knowing overwhelmed the grief. What had happened, and who could tell him? Someone had buried his family. Someone had left a space for him in the row.

Sett rose and turned toward where he had left the mare. She had wandered across the clearing and was carefully snuffing at the little blue dog who was never far from Ria's side. Ria sat on a boulder hugging her knees, dark hair loose over her shoulders, eyes on him.

No shame, Sett thought, no shame for staring at a grieving man and making friends with his horse. He walked straight for her.

"Are you going to sneak up on me everywhere I go?" he demanded.

"I was here when you got here." The girl looked

tired, blue shadows under her large eyes. "The people you looked for?" she asked, nodding at the graves.

"Yes. My family."

"What do they say, the carvings in wood? I always wonder."

Sett sat down on the edge of the boulder and stared back at the headboards.

"They don't say enough. That's my younger brother. He died of the cholera. Next is my father. He was sick too, I guess. I knew about them. But the last ones are my mother and my sister, and the hired man. What happened? Do you know?" Sett leaned over to look the girl in her tired eyes. "Would you tell me if you knew?"

Ria started. The blond man's eyes searched hers. Her heart did a little skip and step. This man was sad; he was alone and he was grieving. Ria wished she could tell him what he needed to know.

"I found the graves one day when I gathered wood. Augie never said anything. I never asked." She looked down at her moccasins.

Sett sighed. The girl would not be much help. He looked at her closer. This morning, she was more quiet and resigned than the badger-woman who had held a gun on him from the cabin. He did not know anything about her but her name. She was obviously not a daughter, yet she seemed somehow in control.

Sett leaned back and watched the morning sun filter into the trees. It was going to be a warm day for so high in the mountains. The bay mare cropped grass eagerly beside them and Sett realized he was hungry, his dinner having gone uneaten the night before.

"I'm going back to camp, get something to eat. You want a ride?" Ria looked surprised, but she nodded as Sett caught up the mare and pulled himself up on her

saddleless back. "Come on." He reached his hand down
and stuck out his foot. Ria grasped his arm, put her neat
moccasin on his large one and swung up behind him as
if they had practiced. The young mare humped her back
at the unusual weight on her hips, and began to roll her
eyes. Ria wrapped her arms around Sett's waist and tried
not to kick the mare. The blue dog whined anxiously as
the mare spun around and Sett crooned to her.

"Hang on." Sett urged the horse across the clearing,
past the row of headboards and up through the pines.

"Where are you going?" Ria glanced back at the trail
down to the cabin.

"We don't want to buck downhill, do we?" The nervous horse trotted out of the grove into the upper hay
meadow. As the way cleared, Sett let her out and the
jolting trot turned into a smooth-flowing run. This was
what the big mare did best. Bred to race, she stretched
her long legs over the spring grass and forgot about
bucking off the strange weight behind Sett. Ria knotted
her fingers in his shirt. She did not want to slip from the
rolling back, and glanced behind to see Coy struggling
to catch up. This man rode firmly balanced on the sleek
mare, his legs long against her. There was no hint of
him being unseated.

The gradual slope of the park whirled past and Sett
guided the mare onto the break of the ridge. She showed
no sign of slowing as they topped the hogback and angled across the face. Ria had ridden, but never like this.
The horse pounded around boulders and holes without
a break in rhythm. The wind whipped Ria's eyes closed.
She clung to Sett as they passed the upper spring, its
dilapidated trough spilling over. Finally at the far edge
of the grassy slope, Sett eased the mare back to a walk.
He circled her once, then headed back down the hill.

Ria slid forward into him as they descended. If she leaned out, she could see the cabin below in the distance. She began to worry about her dog, left so far behind by the leggy mare, then she worried about herself. She tried to let go of Sett and push herself back on the mare, but she only slipped closer to the man.

"Sit still. Your squirming around will set her off again," Sett cautioned over his shoulder. Ria wrapped her arms around his waist.

This was new, this being so close to a man who wasn't Augie. This man's body was hard, the muscles plainly felt. Ria leaned her head between his shoulder blades and inhaled deeply. He had his own unique scent, a mix of sweat and horse and damp cotton.

And he had his own air of distraction. She wondered if he was as conscious of her presence as she was of his. They made their way down the mountain in the early June morning, her body pressed against his, legs fitting with legs, hips moving in unison with the mare. Ria felt peaceful somehow, and that worried her. This Sett Foster was an outlaw, a convicted stage robber, consort of murderers. He was one of Whitey Kennady's band of killers and she was riding double with him, pressed against him like she had only pressed against old Augie.

It worried her.

It worried her most that she was not afraid. It worried her that she could have ridden on and on through this warming spring morning, forgetting about Augie and Ma'am and Carolyn and coming with the house, if only she continued to feel this man next to her. So caught up was she in the sensation of him, that she was startled when he spoke.

"Who are you?"

Ria was silent. That the man would ask her the very

question she had wrestled with all night, the question for which she did not yet have an answer—it stole her tongue. Her silence stretched until the hoof falls of the horse thundered in her ears and Sett finally leaned around and gazed at her over his shoulder.

"What do I have to do to get an answer?" There was no smile.

"I'm Ria . . ." The dark girl hesitated. "I . . . I come with the house."

Sett raised his eyebrows quizzically, but there was no more explanation. "Then you are a new feature since I was here last. Do all houses come with a girl around here?"

Ria flushed. There was way more to the story, but she was not even sure where it began. If he had asked three months ago, she would have known who she was. Three months ago she was Augie's wife; three months ago this was her house. Three months . . .

Sett watched her uneasiness. He did not want to underestimate her. This was the gunman in the cabin after all, the person who had caught him in his moment of vulnerability. She had come out to his camp last night, and waited for him this morning. What did she want? Sett wished she did not want anything, but he knew better. He had enough to worry about without some girl latching on to him. There were questions needing answers; there was grief that needed attending. The whirl of the last day's discoveries left Sett drifting himself. All those years wishing, wanting, trying to get home. Now he was here and none of his questions were answered, only more questions added to the pile. He studied the perplexed brow and downcast eyes of the dark girl who nestled behind him on the bay mare. She had a load of problems too. Maybe he didn't want to know what they were just yet.

Coy caught up with the riders as they entered the hay meadow above the cabin. Sett and Ria had ridden in silence, Ria hugging close, as if Sett might disappear before she decided what to say. The dog's appearance was a relief.

Ria crooned down at the waggle-tailed bitch. Sett listened to her flowing mixture of Sioux and French.

"You're not often out of sight," Sett commented. "That's a good dog."

"Yes, she is a friend." Ria watched as Coy fell in behind the horse.

"I know the feeling."

As they neared the cabin, Sett pulled the horse to a halt. "I need grain. And I need to ask some questions. Millers still have the trading post on the river?"

"Yes."

"Think I'll head in after breakfast. I'll be back before your Augie Johnson returns." Sett reached around and grasped the girl by the belt. "Off you go." He swung her down from the mare's broad back, setting her in the grass next to her blue dog. Ria followed him with her eyes as he rode past the cabin and down to his camp.

Carolyn was waiting when Ria opened the cabin door.

"I had to haul in the water, and you were off gallivanting again with that Foster man. Mama had to start breakfast. What are you up to?" Carolyn eyed Ria suspiciously. "Are you siding with him?"

Ria gave her a look as she slipped past her into the kitchen, where Ma'am was bent over staring into the firebox of the stove. The ashes were piling up in the clean-out box, suffocating the kindling and creating a seeping smoke in the cabin. Ria picked up the ash pail and the small scoop shovel.

"It's about time you showed up, Ria. Carolyn says you're keeping company with that man. How can you be such a hussy! We don't even know why he's here, let alone if he means us harm or good. One would think that even a half-breed like you would have more loyalty to her benefactor." Ma'am pulled herself into that shoulders-back stance that Ria assumed all white women adopted. "August will be so displeased to learn that you have neglected your duties in our time of need."

Ria turned to face the tall woman. Ma'am was wearing a cotton dress, clean still this early in the morning. She and Carolyn had a chest full of cloth dresses, blue and pink and yellow, none of which they wore for more than a day. Ma'am spent all her time sewing the ruffles and pinning the puffed sleeves. It was Ria who washed the laundry every week, Ria who gathered and cooked the meals, Ria who swept the house, then tossed hay to the mules and scratch to the chickens.

She stood next to the warming cookstove and looked up at Ma'am. This woman had no idea of mountain duties, of how life ticked in the wilds of Montana Territory. Ria stared at Augie's wife, his other wife, in her house, telling her what to do.

Anger made the words fly out of her mouth without thinking, a string of Sioux and French that did nothing to dampen her meaning.

"Augie will know you let some stranger ride up behind you. Look, you cannot even make a fire!" Ria slammed the firebox door. "You go back. You die in a week here without someone to take care of you." She finished in American, "Go away. Go back away."

Ma'am's face grew rigid. She grabbed Ria's shoulder with her white hand and gave her a shake.

"You think we can just go back, just like that? Carolyn and I would be gone tomorrow if August would move back to Kentucky, but he won't. How do you think I feel, arriving out here to find this hovel? And you! I have begged August to send you away, but he won't do that either. I know what is going on with you and him. He is not the man I married, not at all. All this Western adventure has corrupted him until he has lost his senses. But he is my husband, *my* husband, do you understand, you little tramp! We were married in the Church with a preacher and a congregation present. And I will not leave without him." Ma'am's pale face was florid and she dug her nails into Ria's shoulder. Carolyn smirked at Ria from the doorway.

"Wait until Papa hears about you and that outlaw, Ria," Carolyn added. "I'm sure he'll appreciate your loyalty then!"

Ria pulled away. Bitterness in her throat, she opened her mouth, but the words were all gone. She glanced at the ash bucket and shovel in her hands, the hot cinders from the stove twinkling. Then she heaved the pail at Ma'am, the fine gray dust pluming into the woman's startled face, and the tiny black coals coating the front of her neatly fitted dress.

FOUR

Sett returned to camp and fried up the trout for breakfast before saddling the mare. Miller's Trading Post was across the valley and the day was heating up. As the trail left the forest and wound out over the sagebrush plain, he let the horse settle into a long walk. It gave him time to think, to mull the past day around in his head and identify the gaps in his knowledge. Five graves, not even dates to hint at what happened. Elizabeth would have been twenty-one this year. She had been a thistle-headed five-year-old when he left.

Sett closed his eyes for a moment. He could see her peeking through the bars of the corral, watching him catch up his little sorrel pony, that night. He'd been angry at her for following him. She stood out there, flannel nightgown dragging in the damp grass and asked in her serious little voice where he was going. Sett had carried her back to the cabin, trying not to answer her question.

"Elizabeth, you go in and get back in bed now. Anyone asks about your nightgown, you tell 'em you went to the outhouse, okay? You don't say nothing about me." He set her down on the doorstep and whispered, "I'll be fine. I'll be back."

"Promise? " Elizabeth had gazed up at him with deep hazel eyes.

"Yes. Yes, I promise." She was the last of his family he would ever see.

The valley spread out ahead of Sett, sage floor sweeping up to the brooding mountains in the West. Thunderheads capped the peaks in preparation for the afternoon storms. The high plains were thriving, vivid flowers sprinkled in with sage and bunchgrass, cottonwoods marking the water canyons with distinct green.

He'd left in the fall, a few days after his thirteenth birthday, to wrangle horses for Whitey Kennady. At least he thought he was going to wrangle horses. It all seemed like the thing to do, Whitey taking him up on the job and Sett wanting to go so bad, wanting to see someplace over the mountains, that he said yes and decided to tell his father later, maybe write him a letter from some faraway town. He'd since learned to think before he acted. But at thirteen, thinking was not what Sett did best.

Tall for his age, long bones grown before the meat could keep up, Sett was like a gangly scarecrow up on his pony. The youthful face that grinned eagerly at Whitey Kennady would mature into the square jaw and watchful eyes of the man, but right then he had been as much of a boy as he ever was. And he had made decisions in that blindness that turned his life to hell. Even now, riding along the trail to Miller's Post the foolishness of that choice haunted him. As if his mother and sister rode by his side, Sett listened to the voices and tried to come up with an explanation.

He'd been good with a horse, and Whitey needed

someone to tend the horses. It was part of Whitey's plan, the part he didn't explain to the boy until they were over the ridge. They'd use the extra horses to outrun the inevitable posse, and Whitey needed Jed and the Tejano with him in the ambush. The kid had known the area too, known where the line cabin was on the divide and the spring hidden in the dry eastern slope of the gray hills. It had been Sett who had gotten them away, by that time finally aware of just what it was he had done, and what would happen to him if he did not use his wits to aid in the escape. He could not give the ghosts a good answer as to why, but he could tell them exactly when the guilt started.

The fine bay mare paused at the top of a coolie then launched herself down the steep bank. Sett sat back in the battered saddle and let her pick her way. There'd not been a horse in Whitey's string equal to the bay mare, but Sett's red pony had done herself proud. Sett had been the only rider without a spare horse; still he had led the small party up to the pass. If it had just been up to the men and beasts, the plan would have worked. But it was fall when Sett left, and winter had been hard on their heels.

Sett rode alone with his ghosts across the alluvial plain studded with boulders and gravel washes. As they neared the creek, the grass grew lush and the cottonwoods offered inviting shade from the sun. The twin ruts of the wagon trail paralleled the rushing stream, as they would for a mile before crossing. Foster Creek carved out a steep bed this high on the mountain, although the altitude was deceiving.

The valley's expanse was broad and shallow, a bowl in the ring of peaks. Even now, in June, snow clung to the divide while Sett sweat dark semicircles under his arms. Winters were treacherous. In the heat of the day, Sett could clearly imagine his mother and sister lying cold and blue, caught out in an unseasonal blizzard. He could picture a buckboard overturned in the rushing crossing of the river. He could envision the sickbed, the one caring for the dying other until both were in the grasp of the cholera, like Ben, or consumption. Torture himself as he would, he found no answers.

The trail finally dipped down into the crossing, and the mare splashed through the clear water and followed the tracks as they left the creek and headed north toward the faint dark patches of settlement that marked Miller's Trading Post in the distance.

Josh Miller had come to the valley about the same time as Moses Foster and his family, but he had no plans of homesteading. Instead, he had carved a soddy out of the cut bank of the river, and shortly opened a store. Miller was the closest supplier of flour, and calico and nails to the homesteaders in the mountains. Sett remembered making the trip with his father to the sparse post. They would eat at Miller's table, amply fortified by Abigail Miller's biscuits, then Sett would wander off to look at the horses with Josh's son Poke while the men discussed business. The single sod cabin had been expanded to two, and Miller's Post had survived as the community store where the nearest customer rode over an hour to get there.

As Sett approached the cluster of soddies, he could see that it had grown in the years he had been gone. The two original dugouts were flanked by log structures, one a large barn and the other a squat cabin with several rooms. The hitching rail in the yard was empty, but the corral held horses.

Sett splashed across the swift river, wide but not deep,

and rode up to the trough. Dismounting, he removed the bridle so the mare could drink freely from the green water. When she was sated, he led her over to the rail and tied her. Then he turned to the old soddy. It still had the sign over the door, "Miller's Trading Post," and as he peered into the darkness he could make out a row of shelves filled with goods on the walls. Behind the counter in the back, a man waited with his hands down. Sett squinted at the sudden change of light.

"Can I help you?" the man asked.

"Yeah. I'm looking for Josh Miller." Sett stepped on into the dim room.

"Josh ain't around. Who's looking for him?" This clerk seemed a mite touchy, Sett thought. He tried to make out the form of the man behind the planks, but his eyes were still adjusting to the lack of light. "Me. I need some grain for my horse. I'm an old friend of his." Sett walked on into the center of the store and peered at the clerk. Something clicked: that thin black hair, the lively blue eyes—

"Poke! Is that you? It's me, Sett. Sett Foster."

"Sett Foster? Can't be!" Poke Miller stuffed something into the shelf under the counter and sashayed out to stand toe-to-toe with Sett. "Sett! It is you! How long you been back?" Poke reached up, grabbed Sett's shoulders and gave him a shake.

"Just got here yesterday. Things sure have changed. You running this enterprise now?" Old Poke hadn't grown much since they were thirteen. He was still a wiry fellow with an engaging smile, only the years had filled him out. Poke had never been called poky; his name had been hung on him instead by Sett's own father: *You never know what that kid is going to come up with next;*

he's sure a pig in a poke, that one. Sett grinned down at his old friend.

"Well, yes, I am. What do you know?" Poke led him over to the counter and produced a brown bottle and two glasses. "You been out to the homestead?"

Sett leaned on the planks and frowned. "Yeah, been home, but I don't know nothing." He accepted the drink with a nod. "Matter of fact, one reason I'm here, besides supplies, is answers. I supposed Josh would know."

Now it was Poke's turn to wrinkle his brow. "Gee, Sett, there's a lot has happened. Pa died two winters back, Ma is living with us. I'm a married man, Sett, got two little girls. I've been running the post for a few years now. It's been good." Poke paused to consider his friend's travel-worn clothes and stained hat. "What about you? How long you been out?"

Sett sipped at the whiskey thoughtfully. He'd been out a long time, too long. It was hard to explain even to himself why he hadn't come straight home. He'd intended to, but somehow the adjustment to life took more than he'd expected. He was released a man in size and years, but green as any boy to the workings of society. The one thing he knew, he didn't want to go back to jail. That in itself had been an undertaking. Seemed everyone knew the story of Whitey Kennady and the Boy Stage Robber, and had an opinion of Sett before they even met him. Sett kept moving, kept learning, and kept trying to come up with an explanation that would satisfy himself and his mother. He never did.

"Poke, I could tell you the long story, and I will someday if you really want to hear it, but the truth is I've been out four years. I finally got home and there are these two strange women and a breed girl living in my cabin, and a cemetery full of my family. And I didn't know." Sett drained the glass and thumped it back to the counter. Poke offered the bottle again, but he shook his head and continued. "What happened? What happened to Mama and Elizabeth?" He turned to his boyhood friend. Poke looked him square in the face.

"Sett, I sure don't want to be the one to tell you this, but I guess I'm elected. We had some rough years. I guess it's still pretty rough, but for a while there, with the nearest law in Helena, there were more wild-ass thieves and robber bands than good citizens in these parts. It was, oh, about four years ago, I guess. November. Your mama and Elizabeth hadn't been into the post and Pa got to worrying. Your mama had been waiting for a bolt of chambray, so when we got it, Pa rode out to the homestead with it. He found them, Sett. They'd been there awhile. He said it looked like they had tried to get into the cabin, but they didn't make it. The hired man was shot in the back." Poke paused and rubbed his hand from cheek to brow. "Sett, I suppose you want all the details?"

"You might as well tell me."

"Rose, your mama, she was in the doorway. She been hit, hit hard on the head. Crushed her skull . . . probably a rifle butt," Poke stopped again. He poured himself another drink and swallowed deep. "It wasn't a pretty sight. The house was ransacked, clothes and cookware thrown about. Chest turned over." Sett could picture the hope chest, Rose's prize possession, overturned with her linen, her wedding dress, her daguerreotypes of her parents, strewn across the floor. He shut his eyes tight but the vision remained.

"Elizabeth?" he finally managed to say. Poke looked away at the display of sewing needles and thread at the end of the counter.

''They . . . kept her awhile, Sett. Pa found her in the barn, stripped naked, tied out in a stall.''

Sett turned and staggered out of the soddy. He could taste the bile in his throat and his only thought was to get out of the dark little room. Outside he gulped air like a trout on a creek bank. Poke followed cautiously.

''Sett, are you all right? I'm sorry. It was a bad time around here. There was problems over by Verdy too. An immigrant family killed. The townspeople in Helena formed a vigilante committee, got some of them. Hung 'em on Main Street.''

Sett was staring off at the thunderheads circling the divide. ''They raped her,'' he stated.

''Yes.'' Poke started to say more, but a look at Sett's face stopped him. Maybe his friend didn't need to know everything.

''Why?''

''They were looking for the gold. No one's ever found it, but that's what they all were looking for. Seemed like all the rabble in Montana came through here, dangerous men, no morals. Pa tried to talk your mama into moving down here closer, but she loved that house.'' Poke shook his head. ''Look, Sett, didn't you get the letter? I wrote you.'' Sett could not look at his childhood friend. ''It was a long time ago. There was nothing you could have done.''

Sett continued to watch the afternoon storm gather itself over the Rockies. The clouds shifted, gray tendrils straying down into the canyons, then silver highlights rimming the scalloped edges. Looked like they would get weather this evening. Sett was ready for it.

A childish shriek broke the stillness. From the cabin, a young girl in blue calico raced across the yard, towing a smaller child by the hand.

"Daddy! Daddy! Momma says to come to dinner."
The child slid to a stop at Poke's feet. She glanced
briefly at the man contemplating the mountains. "And
she says to invite Mr. Foster to eat with us." The child
leaned closer to her father and whispered, "Gramma
says he's an old friend. Is he, Daddy?"

"Yes, darlin'. Sett and I are old friends. Tell your
mama we'll be there in a moment." The girl headed
back to the cabin, still leading the younger one. Poke
turned to Sett.

"Why don't you unsaddle your horse and give her a
feed, and come meet my family? Ma will never forgive
you if you don't say hello. She was your mama's best
friend to the end." Sett did not move. Poke stepped up
beside him, standing shoulder to armpit with his buddy,
the outlaw. "Sett, I know it hurts. I cried when I dug
your mother and sister's graves. I cried when I dug my
pa's grave. Take my word for it, grief is easier when it's
shared." He spun on his heel and headed for his cabin.

Ria sat up in the deer park behind the cabin. The little
clearing was a fresh green this early in the summer, and
the marshy spot trickled down over the rocky edge. She
had fully intended to run from the cabin and keep running, but hours later found herself only as far away as
this familiar spot.

She needed to think. It was time to leave. Augie
would be home tomorrow and the return of the outlaw
would keep him occupied, but she did not have a horse,
or any possessions other than her clothes, and she did
not have a place to go. Her mother had gone west three
years ago, with her new man, hoping that her oldest
daughter was securely provided for.

It had been the best choice, the only choice for the

second widow of the trapper LaBlanc. Winter was fast approaching, and the memories of thin broth and thin children had driven Sweetgrass Woman to the trading post on the Missouri with her daughter and infant son. The fall gathering of trappers, mountain men from the Rockies and pole boaters from the river was the largest gathering of humanity that Ria had ever seen.

She had hidden in the lodge and cared for her baby brother while Sweetgrass Woman put on her best dress and painted her face, taking care with the laboriously beaded leggins, and went out among the variety of men to find a new one to care for her family.

It had not taken long. Sweetgrass Woman was pretty, and the lean year since LaBlanc had left to check his trap lines and never returned had kept her slender. She moved in with a grizzly man named Ross, and began preparing jerky for the long trip to his stomping grounds in the Sawtooth Range.

The noise and confusion of the rendezvous had kept Ria inside most of the time, and her mother had encouraged it. The young woman, with her freckled skin and wild hair, was too tempting a sight to be out alone in the crowd of men and their whiskey. But the new man had not seen the girl as a daughter to be protected; he saw a valuable asset. Near the end of the gathering when some of the trappers were already setting off for their lonely winters in the mountains, Ross entered the tent and ordered Sweetgrass Woman to dress Ria and paint her face.

"She is too young," her mother had protested.

"She is close enough, and this white man is rich. He wants a young wife for his homestead." Ross motioned impatiently. "He will take care of her, and he will pay well. Now, hurry up." Sweetgrass Woman gave Ria her own beaded poncho and moccasins, although they were too big, and oiled her brown hair until the wispy curls around her face were sleek. She painted three yellow tears under each eye and three black lines radiating from the full lower lip to the chin.

"That looks like mourning paint," the big man had complained, but in this Sweetgrass Woman ignored him. Ria tried not to cry as she followed Ross across the campsite. She looked back once for her mother, but the woman had gone back inside the lodge and pulled the flap closed. She could hear the strange voices of the mountain men, some in the languages she could understand, calling out to her guide as they passed.

"What you got there, Ross?"

"How come we never seen her before?"

"*Que bella.*"

Ria stepped quickly to keep up. She was being sold as a wife, something that would have happened eventually. It was her fate. She could only have hope that the rich white man with a homestead would be a kind husband, would provide for her and not beat her undeservedly. Her heart thumped with every step, like the drum of the mourning dance, but her feet walked steadily toward August Johnson, of Kentucky.

That Augie was neither rich nor successful did not bother her; that he occasionally drank too much whiskey and used her hard she assumed was the right of a husband. Even the angry cuff when she had misread his wishes, in the early days before she had learned the American words, was no worse than she had seen in the lodge of her childhood. Ria quickly learned to have the meal on the table when Augie came in and coffee ready when he dragged himself out of bed in the morning. Even the strange language was mastered enough to keep the peace, and Augie, all his needs met, mostly left her alone. Ria spent her days gathering and preparing, cooking and mending for the two of them, with plenty of time to explore the woods around the homestead and to fish in the stream. She did it without thought. A woman's life spread out before her without her once ever counting the years.

All that had changed. It was the white women, the wife and daughter from Kentucky. How could Ma'am be first wife and she no wife at all? Augie would not explain. She no longer ran her lodge.

Ria sat in the sun-dappled clearing and hugged her knees. Coy was off scouting in the low brush and Ria could hear her digging after a gopher. Tomorrow. Augie would be back tomorrow. Could she walk to Miller's Post? It was the nearest place to find a freighter, but she could meet Augie coming in. And Poke Miller would know her. The old trail north, over the mountains? She did not know the way, and alone without provisions—it was risky.

Her thoughts returned to the outlaw, Sett Foster. He knew the way across the mountains. The sky was clouding up, evening thunderstorms hustling across the valley. She stood and whistled for Coy. The plan was unclear, but she would return to the cabin, collect her things and wait.

It didn't occur to Sett until he was washing his face at the enamel pan outside the kitchen. Poke's daughter had used his name. Someone had recognized him from the house.

He examined himself in the mirror over the washstand. He didn't feel at all like the boy who had visited here so long ago. It was like some stranger had assumed his name and ridden his life off in a stampede, then handed it back for him to cool out. The recognition was a surprise; he'd been worried about his own mother knowing him, but who he was must be apparent from rods away.

He ran his fingers through his hair, and wiped at the stubble on his jaw, making a mental note to get one of these mirrors from Poke when he collected his supplies. Hat in hand, Sett climbed the two steps to the porch and paused at the open door.

Delicious scents wafted out of the room, and the long table was set with real plates and a big bowl of biscuits covered with a towel. Poke was carving away at a haunch of roast and his daughter was delivering a bowl of fresh butter to the table. It was a prosperous scene, and for a moment Sett felt like backing out the door and disappearing into the mountains again, but a voice from the end of the table nearest the stove stopped him.

"Settler Paul, come sit here by me so I can see you." The woman in the chair reached her frail hand up and beckoned. Her gray hair was contained by a white lace cap, her shoulders wrapped by a bright flowered shawl. She was blind, her eyes milky from cataracts. Sett wondered how she knew he was there, how she knew it was him. He swallowed against the thickness in his throat. Having hung his hat on a hook by the door, he walked around the table and took her hand.

"Auntie Abby," he started, but then could not say anything more. She was so old! He remembered Abigail Miller waving her big wooden spoon at Poke and him when they rushed through the kitchen. He remembered her scolding him for not washing behind his ears before sitting down to dinner. He remembered her sitting with his mother out on the porch comparing recipes. The blue-skinned hand in his had a surprising grip, and she pulled him down close to her face.

"Yes, I'd know you anywhere, you are so like your father." Poke's mother released his hand and reached up to pat his cheek with cool fingers. "It is good to have you back. You are still a horseman; I could hear your spurs." Sett was silent. He could think of nothing to say, and was afraid to even try through the choking hold on his throat.

Just then a young woman swept in from the sleeping room, carrying the toddler.

"Sett, I'd like you to meet my wife, Samantha." Poke broke the stillness. The woman smiled warmly at Sett.

"Welcome, Mr. Foster. These are our daughters, Jeanette and our oldest, Gail." Samantha Miller put the baby down on the bench and hurried to bring the remaining serving bowls to the table. "Please eat, everyone, before it gets cold."

Sett filled his plate automatically and passed dishes across to Poke, who served his mother. He hoped Poke and his family would not wonder too much at his silence, but words refused to come. He was surrounded by people who treated him like family, people who nearly were family, after all these years. After a few bites of the steaming biscuits and savory roast, though, he realized how long it had been since he had eaten at a well-prepared table. As the potatoes and small carrots, roasted in the pan with the meat, disappeared from his plate, and the gravy was soaked up with a biscuit, Samantha passed him the serving bowls again with a smile. Poke sliced another piece of the roast and slid it onto his plate. Sett thanked him without looking up and continued to eat like the man with miles behind him. Only after the third plateful did Sett look around and see the

Millers watching him with indulgent smiles. The girls stared wide-eyed as he mopped up the last of the juice on his plate, and Poke grinned.

"I'd forgotten how you could eat," he laughed, "maybe I should have shot the other elk!"

Sett flushed with embarrassment and mumbled to Samantha, "Thank you, ma'am. I'm sorry for not being better company. The meal was delicious."

"Anytime, Sett. Now, if you would like to sit on the porch with Mother Abby, I'll bring the coffee and pie out there. Gail, will you help me?" She stood and began clearing the table. The old woman rose and tapped her way to the door with her cane. Sett followed her, again feeling at loose ends to be dropped down into this scene. Abby settled herself in a rocker and her hazy eyes focused off across the valley as if she could see.

"There's weather comin' in," she commented.

"Yeah, there's a thunderhead sitting up on Black Peak. We'll get some rain tonight." Sett stretched to ease the fullness in his belly.

"Are you staying with the Johnsons?"

"No, I'm in the camp down by the beaver ponds. I don't think I'm much welcome and their man is off to Verdy till tomorrow." Sett checked on the mare finishing off her feed in the corral. "A little rain won't hurt me; I've been out in it a lot lately."

"Well, the least that outfit could do is let you stay in the barn," Abby snorted. Sett closed his eyes against the vision that summoned.

"I don't think I could do that," he finally said. Abigail turned and held him in her chalky gaze. She could barely make out the shape of her best friend's son leaning against the porch rail: a big man, strong and well made like his father.

"Poke told you everything?"

"He told me what he thought I could stand," Sett said bitterly.

The old woman shook her head. "It's a bad time. All those men loose after the war with nothing to do but go on killing and killing. Drifters, fortune seekers. The vigilantes from over in Helena hanging men in the streets."

Abigail strained to discern more of Sett's features than his silhouette. His clothes were travel worn and his hair shaggy—this she knew from Samantha's description of him in the yard. He was riding a fine big horse too, a better horse than he looked like he could afford. They had watched him riding across the valley, and called the girls to the cabin while Poke went to mind the store. It was their normal procedure with strangers. But watching Poke's easy familiarity had led to closer observation. Samantha had described him and Abigail sorted out who he must be, or at least who he had been. Her son seemed comfortable with having Sett Foster in his home, but Abigail Miller wished she could see him, really see him, and look into his eyes.

"Where have you been, Sett?" she said kindly. "What will you do now?" Sett looked at the lined face peering up at him. She was asking in a friendly way what everyone he'd met since getting out really wanted to know: Who was he and what did he want? The answers were shifting so quickly that he didn't know himself, but he could not avoid this question from the woman so close to his mother.

"Been riding around, I guess, trying to figure it out," he offered.

"Figure what out?"

"Life. How life works. I mean, here in the world, not in prison. I know how life in prison works." Sett paused.

"I missed a lot of it, and it can't be replaced. I hoped it could, but now it can't."

"No, it can't," the old woman agreed. "But even if you never figure out life, it continues. Forgive and go on, Sett."

"My family was murdered for nothing. I can't forgive that."

"You can forgive yourself."

Sett studied the darkening sky again. He had a sudden need to be back out in the mountains, into the wild spaces where his heart could answer his own questions. "I'd better get my supplies and head back to camp. Thank you for the hospitality, Aunt Abby."

FIVE

It was late, time for supper, and that damn girl wasn't back. Carolyn went into the yard and yelled for her, but got no response. Her mother was starting the fire, but with the gathering storm darkening the sky, Carolyn noticed that the wood box was empty. She heaved a disgusted sigh. Someone would have to chop wood. She headed for the cabin.

"No sign of Ria, Mother, and we're out of wood." The older woman was bent over, looking into the firebox of the stove. She straightened with one hand on her back.

"I cannot possibly chop firewood!" She waved her hand at the smoky stove. "We are out of kindling too. She was supposed to bring that yesterday."

"Yesterday she was spending time with that wild man, Foster." Carolyn crossed her arms and glared out the window. "She's probably there now."

Mrs. Johnson joined her daughter at the window. This was a sticky wicket, as her daddy would say, to be so dependent on one's husband's mistress. Constance Johnson tightened her lips at the thought. She should have listened to Daddy; August really was no good. To have sprung this on them after abandoning them for years . . . She thought back. Poor Carolyn hardly knew her father, raised as she had been in her grandparents' home after August disappeared. Now here they were, stuck in a strange wild place, still without August most of the time, and at the mercy of an illiterate half-breed girl who thought she was August's real wife! Constance shook her head at the mysteries of life.

"Well, it's getting dark. If that little tramp thinks she is going to behave like that then show up for supper, she is wrong. It's time we put an end to this." Constance marched outside and examined the woodpile. "Carolyn, bring in as many of those sticks as you can. August will be home tomorrow afternoon. Surely you and I can survive until then. When August finds out about this, he will have to send her away."

"We are going to lock her out?" Carolyn seemed cheered at the prospect.

"Yes. This is my house and I will no longer have that girl and her smelly dog under my roof!" Constance headed back inside.

Poke walked with Sett as far as the river. When they reached the gravel bank, they paused and watched the spring melt-off roil past. They had been silent since Sett loaded his saddlebags and insisted on paying with the last of his poker earnings.

"You know, Sett, you're welcome to stay with us." Sett gazed off across the river to the Cottonwoods. He shook his head. Poke continued, "I don't know what you got planned, but I think you should know that there's some around that won't be happy to find you're back. The vigilante committee is pretty determined to run the country their way. Your name is on their list.''

"I haven't been welcome anywhere since I left here. I've paid my debt, several times over. I just wanted to see my people. Is that too much to ask?"

"No. Knowing you like I do, I think they're wrong. But the story, it won't die. It's that gold. It's never been found. There's only one member of the Kennady band left, and that's you. Old August Johnson is not going to be happy to find you here." Poke cast an eye up to the threatening sky.

Sett frowned. "What the hell is this gold you keep talking about?"

"You know, Sett. The gold from the stage. Whitey Kennady's gold. It's never been found. They say he cached it here."

Poke watched the tall man's eyes cloud over, like a storm covering his face. "There is no damned gold." Sett spat and urged the mare down into the river.

The ride back to the camp was mostly uphill, and Sett let the horse trot until they reached the steep crossing of Cottonwood Creek. The sky was dark with clouds, and the wind stirred the leaves. An occasional streak of sunlight played under the thunderheads as the sun disappeared behind the Rockies, but Sett neither noticed nor hurried. There didn't seem to be much reason to hurry anymore. He hadn't hurried when it could have mattered. Now it was too late.

He'd hung around Sheridan for months after being released from prison, managing to land a job breaking colts and waiting for Pablo to get out. But his cell mate did not show and Sett decided that he must have headed straight back for Mexico. Then the slow wandering journey began, from job to job, saloon to saloon, whore to whore. He had stumbled around, trying to reclaim his

body, know his soul, meet the man known as Settler
Paul Foster. Meanwhile his mother was being bludg-
eoned to death in the doorway of her home and his sister . . .

Sett was pelted out of his brooding by the first big
drops of rain as he started up the canyon. He already
appreciated the tarpaulin that Poke had given him, one
big enough to go over the pole tent frame at the camp.
It was dark when he arrived, but the tent was up and his
gear stashed inside quickly. He built a small fire and
hobbled the mare so she could find a sheltering bank or
grove, then sat in the opening of the tent with a cup of
coffee and cigarette makings.

The tent frame was permanent, made of saplings
lashed to the trees that edged the clearing. Someone had
ditched around it, and Sett watched the water rush off
toward the creek while he sat in the relative dry and
smoked. The summer storm poured down: huge drops
of water so heavy that they fell straight to earth, and
thunder rolling closer. Sett pulled off his damp boots
and put them under the end of the bedroll. He pulled the
blanket up around his shoulders, then up over his head
like old man Talking Crow when the stories turned sad.
As if the old Blackfeet leader were sitting there beside
Sett's fire lamenting the changes to his world, speaking
in his soft tongue about his daughter marrying away to
a white man, and the traditional hunting grounds being
taken over by the miners and railroad tracks. Now the
loss from years ago visited Sett, a darkness held out by
the woven wool of the trade blanket.

It suited his mood, wrapped in layers of blanket and
tent and storm. He finished his cigarette and looked out
to check on his horse. She was barely discernible under
the thick trees, rump to the rain and big mare ears out

flat. Sett pulled the flap closed and removed his damp clothing to dry in the foot of his bed, then slid into the bedroll.

The storm was right over him now, lightning cracking into the thunder. Each bolt illuminated the pale canvas of the tent, casting tree shadows on the walls. Sett remembered huddling on the pallet with his brother and sister, the three children awakened by a summer thunderstorm. Mama had made hot chamomile tea, and they sat on the boys' shared bed and shivered each time the skies shook the cabin. Their father sat at the table, talking in his deep, calm voice about safety in storms, about not standing under a lone tree, or out in the meadow where the bolts of white light could fry you down to your boot tops. He reminded his sons to get down off the horse, or the hay rake, if they were working when a storm hit, and he looked at Sett and said, "You keep an eye out and help your little sister. She's too young to know what to do by herself."

Then he had told tales of floods and rain in Minnesota, of canals overflowing and mules stranded on flat levee dikes, and funny stories about his mother, Sett's grandmother, gathering up all the chickens and keeping them in the bedroom. Little downy-haired Elizabeth would fall asleep on Sett's lap, quivering in her dreams as the thunder moved off over the Cottonwoods. Sett had never known his grandmother, or the Minnesota farm of his father's youth. He was born in the Dakotas, on the journey west. Both the first child, and the first native Westerner, his father had christened him Settler Paul Foster, for he would be the generation to settle the wild, to build and grow in an untouched land.

A loud rumble from the storm shook Sett back to his reality. The wind was whipping at the tent canvas, the slender aspens along the creek rustling their spring green leaves madly. He sighed, and concentrated on the commotion of nature ranting outside. He could not cry, could not heave and throw and scream. Because if he started, if he began to loosen what was in his chest, he was afraid he could not stop, so he lay still and let the mountains do it for him.

At some point in the journey, Coy took the lead and Ria followed simply because she could not see any further ahead in the slashing rain. Each flash of lightning cast confusing shadows among the dense grove of young trees. Somewhere downhill was the creek. If she could find it, she would follow the bank, but right now, Coy's guiding tail was all she could see.

Water squished from her moccasins and ran down her hair into her eyes. She did not have her heavy robe coat or the wool blanket Augie had bought for her. She did not have anything at all, because they had taken it from her! Locked out of the house. Told to sleep in the barn. Ria had not believed it. She had pounded on the cabin door and tapped on the shuttered window, but that was all they would say. The rain was starting in earnest, cold and drenching. She grabbed a piece of kindling and began smacking the door with it.

"You can't do this! This is my house."

Coy began whining and trying to dig under the door. One of the shutters opened slightly. Ma'am poked her broad nose out the crack.

"We can and we have! This is not your house, it is August's and his family's."

"I am First Wife. It is my house. Open the door." Ria grabbed for the shutter, but Ma'am slammed it shut, catching Ria's fingers. She pulled them out, leaving skin and blood behind. The pain staggered her for a moment, then she headed for the barn. Under the eaves of the horse shelter, she paused to suck at the damaged finger and glare back at the cabin with the light leaking out around the one window and the door. This was enough. She was not going to sleep in the barn like some farm animal while those two slept in her house.

So she had nothing, not even a dry bed of hay in the barn, but then maybe she had had nothing before.

The canyon below the cabin clearing was thick with growth—willows at the bank, aspens and cottonwoods at their appropriate elevations, wild rose and choke-cherry tangling underneath. The trails were along the bank, winding in the willows, sometimes right at the edge of the creek. Fishing trails. Ria had discovered them the first day she was at the homestead. Someone had regularly fished this creek, had stepped enough times on the moss-covered rocks to grind that moss off. But they had been unused for some time. She followed them all; they led her to the best trout ponds. They showed her someone's favorite beaver dam, and the best place to lean against a tree and catch the warm late afternoon sun while your catch stayed fresh in the rock weir at the bank of the ripples. Here in the dark, though, with the lightning playing games with her senses and the rain making a lake of the air, just to recognize one of those trails would be a miracle.

Coy seemed to know where she was going. The trees began to space out, and the brushy edge of the creek came into sight. There were the stepping stones which were normally easy to cross but were now washed over by the muddy deluge of the storm. Coy paused at the bank, looking across and narrowing her eyes. Then she waded into the rushing stream.

Ria splashed in with her, afraid that Coy would not wait for her to consider getting even wetter. The water came just to her knees, but was swift and cold. She didn't even try to step on the crossing stones—they were slick. Clutching her mashed hand to her belly, she trudged through the little stream. Coy paused just long enough to shake on the other side, then chose a trail and trotted off into the darkness.

There hasn't been any thunder for a while now, Ria thought; maybe it is moving away. But just then a double crack of lightning and simultaneous boom of thunder nearly knocked her to the ground. The roaring of the downpour filled her head and she reached up with her good hand to shield her eyes. The next flash of lightning confirmed what she'd thought she saw before. She was in the old camp clearing and there was a tent set up over the pole frame at the edge of the aspen grove. Coy was heading toward it.

The scratching at the canvas by his head startled Sett. He reached up and slid the long knife from the sheath, then rolled quietly until his hand was on the rifle alongside the bedroll. He waited, concentrating on the tent flap so hard that the wild sounds of the storm faded to static. The scratching came again, this time much more insistent. A bright strike threw a shadow on the tent wall. It was a coyote, or a small wolf. Sett fingered the rifle. Then there was another flash, and another shadow joined the first, a shadow of a person crouching. Sett let go of the rifle and lifted the knife as the flap was shaken loose from the outside and the breed girl's blue bitch nosed her way into the tent. Just behind her was Ria, dripping water.

"What the hell are you doing here?" Sett hissed. He did not put down the knife.

Ria knelt down by the bedroll and wiped water out of her face with her hand. "They locked me out of my house, those women. They locked me out with nothing. They are trying to kill me."

Sett relaxed a bit.

"So why'd you come here? I'm not going up there and make them let you back in."

"No. I want to stay here, with you." Ria tried to see his face in the dark. He leaned over and slid the knife back into the sheath. The dog was already making a bed in the corner of the tent. He knew he would not throw them back out into the weather, but it bothered him just the same. Entertaining young women in the night generally had appeal, but not tonight. Not when a bloody and crushed vision soaked into his mind every time he closed his eyes. He could see this girl had problems, but he did not want to share them.

Ria pushed her hair away from her face. The outlaw Sett Foster was being very quiet. Maybe he would not let her stay. She shivered in the drenched doeskin poncho, water still puddling in her moccasins. She kept the injured hand close to her lest she bump it on something. What would she do, where could she go, if he chased her out of his tent?

"Let us stay. I will lay with you. I know what to do." She tried to untie the thongs at the neck of her poncho with her good hand.

"You know what to do, huh?" he said speculatively. Although she couldn't see him between the lightning, Ria could tell he was looking at her with that same eyebrow-raised expression as when he asked about her dog barking, or if girls came with all the cabins.

"Yes, yes, I do. I . . ." Her teeth were beginning to chatter.

"Just where did you learn what to do?"

"Augie showed me." In a brief flash she could see Sett leaning back in the bedroll with his arms crossed behind his head, right hand relaxed next to the knife sheath. The blankets were pulled up to his chin. He looked comfortable and warm. His hair was dry, while hers was still plastered to her neck and dripped down her spine. She tugged harder on the knot in the thong.

In the pitch blackness, she felt the cold, flat steel of his knife against her fingers. "Let me cut the knot," he said. She took her hand away. The back of the knife slid up her throat, the blade catching the thong and slicing it neatly. Ria pulled the poncho off over her head. Next she sat and removed her moccasins and leggins, and finally the skirt. She groped in the blackness for the edge of the blankets, and slipped under as quickly as she could. There was warmth from where Sett had been, and she burrowed down into it. She tried to keep her shuddering body away from his until she warmed up. *No one likes a chilly woman,* Augie had laughed during the long Montana winter, but now she wondered if she would ever be warm again.

Having the girl crawl into his bed was like finding a trout in it. Sett was tempted to cringe away from her clammy skin, but her shivering would not cease and he began to worry about her. Maybe she was dangerously chilled, although this was a June storm and fairly warm as Montana weather goes. He reached over and rubbed her shoulder. Her skin was damp, the muscles tight. He moved closer, dropping his arm across her and hugging her to his warmth. He thought he could feel goose bumps, thought he could hear her intake of breath as he pulled her closer.

"I know what to do." Ria rolled to face him.

"You'll do what I tell you," Sett answered. Ria tried to see his eyes in the blackness. There was nothing except the sound of his voice and the warmth of his hand now roving gently on her back.

"What?"

"Go to sleep."

Ria lay very tense until the warmth emanating from his body found its way into hers, melting the fear and anger and leaving her very tired. She did not remember when the thunder moved away over the mountain, or when the last bolt of lightning lit the sky.

Sett noticed it all, lying awake in the night with his arm around the breed girl.

SIX

Muldoon always awoke as if he had never been asleep, pale eyes instantly taking in the surroundings. Lately it had been cotton pillowcases, sunlight coming through the shades and red hair. Today it was a dark stain of rain soaking through the slatted bottom of Augie Johnson's wagon. He had seen to it that he was on the high end. Even rocks under his bedroll were better than the rivulets of water that were working their way under Johnson's bed. Still the oaf slept on.

Sunrise was a ways, but the sky was lightening and the clouds had fled. The downpour of the night before remained only as a drip overhead and muddy going in the near future.

No point in going back to sleep. Muldoon aimed a kick at Johnson's backside.

"Hey, Johnson. Make some coffee." The lump under the neighboring blankets groaned, and Muldoon poked him again. "Get up."

Johnson muttered something about the mud in his

soogan, and he rolled from under the wagon and began shuffling around the damp firepit.

Muldoon hated this cold country. Maybe he was spoiled by the fineries afforded officers, or just had the thin blood of the South in his veins, but sleeping under wagons and consorting with men in bearskin coats caused him to shiver inwardly. He was not meant to be a poor desperado. It was warm, they said, down in South America. He bribed himself with that thought.

He had slept fully dressed, and twisted his mouth in distaste as he stood and shook out his clothes. From the saddlebag he extracted a small kit, and swabbed at his teeth with a tiny brush and combed wax through his mustache. He studied the countryside, the roll of the plains and the vibrant green of the new grass. The ground squished under his boots, reminding him that last night's rain had fallen on already saturated ground.

"How is the river crossing going to be?" Muldoon inquired as he poured the thick coffee into his cup.

Augie grunted. "Wet, but there is usually extra horses at the post there, if you feel like paying Miller for their loan." Miller actually had a cable ferry, but it involved unloading the wagon, so Augie had always taken his chances with the ford. And this time he was more heavily loaded, what with Connie's shopping list and all. He stared morosely into his coffee cup. "Well, better get a move on. Could be a long day." He jammed his felt on his head and shook the coffee grounds into the fire.

The going was not bad along the tops of the swales, the puddles standing on the exposed gravel. In the coulee bottoms was a different matter, and the wagon slid down the ruts of tracks nearly out of control. Augie was saving his breath for cursing at the mules, and Muldoon rode ahead so as not to be splattered with the mud flung by the wheels. The road dipped down into the river's valley, and Muldoon would hardly have recognized it until Augie paused on the next rise and pointed.

"There's my place, Cap'n. Up that canyon behind the little bald knob."

Muldoon fished around in his coat, pulling out the collapsible tube of the monocular. He studied the distant canyon, still not quite sure that he would have found it alone. He had not looked back when he left.

"How much longer?" he asked as he put the eyeglass back in his coat.

"Depends on how long it takes us to get through the river. Should be there by dinner." Augie swatted the mules with the reins.

On the journey out, Muldoon had crossed the river below the post, the water being low in the late fall. He had hurried, following the two other men who'd decided that west was a safer escape than north. It had landed him in Helena, right in the middle of a riot, as the vigilantes marched toward the jailhouse with their torches and rope. Muldoon had slipped away from his companions, grabbed up a torch and helped hang two Indians, one an old man. By morning, cleaned up and freshly shaved, he boarded the train to San Francisco.

He was amazed to be back. As far as his eyes could see there were trees and grassland, rocks and sand and sky, and not a single decent hotel, or bar of soap, or shot of bourbon to be had. There was only Johnson, a man Muldoon had hoped to see the last of that cold November night. But maybe that was luck. Maybe Johnson would be an asset, instead of just an ass.

"So I suppose you have searched the cabin?" Muldoon finally asked.

"Yeah, and the barn and the root cellar and the old outhouse. The locals say it's hid up in the mountains, though." Augie spat at the rump of the off mule. "They say the boy knew the old trails up through the pass."

"If the locals know all about it, how come none on them ever found it?" Muldoon's horse picked his way around a sumpy spot, and the wagon wheel squished its way right through, leaving a rut nearly a foot deep.

"Well, the only real local I talks to is old Bearhat, the trapper, but he knows Miller, and Miller was close with the boy."

"So if the boy was around, Miller'd know?" Muldoon gazed down on the distant cluster of buildings that marked Miller's Post and the river ford. Beyond, the long slopes of the valley slid up into the rumple of the mountains. Huge country.

"I guess. Ain't like Miller and I talk." Augie pulled his hat down and scowled. "He ain't been friendly."

Great, Muldoon thought. Johnson had alienated the only reliable source on Sett Foster. Surely Foster was headed this way. Last gossip had him disappearing into the Beartooths, after that card game. Story of that one had spread from card table to card table. The Boy Stage Robber was out of prison and scrambled himself a rifle and a big Thoroughbred horse, and was headed who knows where, but all likely back to the wilderness to retrieve his loot. Or so the card-table tales went.

Muldoon sighed, noiseless in the warming air. This would be the last chance to find that gold, and after so many years—but what god-awful big country it was!

Poke was watching for the wagon, and he noticed the black speck as it crested the rise, but the horseman accompanying it caused him pause. It wasn't unusual to see a rider moving along with a freighter. There was safety in numbers out here, but old Johnson usually traveled alone.

The river had receded but the earth was soaked, and a small cut bank had developed overnight on the far edge of the ford. Poke meant to go over later with a shovel and improve his road. He wondered if Johnson would try to drive the team through, and anticipated the work of repairing the bog the heavy wagon would create if he did.

Johnson had been right, the ford looked difficult, and Miller was standing in his doorway with barely a flicker of his eyes to reveal that he saw his neighbor driving through the yard. The door to the soddy hut trading post was closed, and the curtains on the cabin twitched as if someone were peeking out.

Muldoon rode ahead to the ford, his horse's hooves stirring the mushy gravel on the beach of the gentle drop. The water was just over the horse's knees, but swift and muddy from the rain. Augie never even paused, but smacked the mules down into the river. His cursing rose above the water and the mules lunged across and hit the far bank running. Then it all stopped.

The wagon sunk in the silt of the cut bank, like an anchor dragging the team. Muldoon slid his horse back down to the struggling mules, dropping a rope on the near mule's neck and pulled from his saddle, but the wagon only sank deeper and Johnson's voice grew uglier as his face turned red.

"Johnson, stop, for Crissakes." Muldoon's own pale face was colored with the bright spots of anger. "You're only making it worse." The mules fought for their footing on the slick bank, and the wagon began to lean to one side. Johnson leaped down out of the seat and got behind the wagon in the water.

"Push, Cap'n, push."

Muldoon sat on the horse, sneering down at the fruitless efforts of the ox in the mud. He looked back across the ford at the buildings and the man who still stood on his porch, watching the show with his arms crossed. No way Muldoon was going to wallow around in the water, when an extra team was right there. He urged his horse back across the river.

Poke Miller watched him come across the yard. A dandy, he thought, the long black coat flapping back to reveal a vest complete with watch fob and gold buttons and, as he drew closer, the slick handle of a revolver in the holster on his hip. Pale face, long and clean shaven but for the neat mustache, glittering glass eyes that remained cold even as the thin lips curled into the semblance of a pleasant expression.

"Good day, sir. As I'm sure you can see, we have need of the rent of your team." Muldoon's words were polite, but a warning buzzed in Poke's head. Too polite to be traveling with Augie Johnson.

"Yeah, I see that. Quite a thunderstorm last night." Poke did not move off the porch. Muldoon waited for a moment, then fished inside his coat and withdrew a small purse.

"How much?" Obviously he was going to have to show his money to get this hick to hitch up the team.

"Two bits." Over in the bog, Augie was flailing away on the back of the mules, each stroke accompanied by loud curses that carried all the way back to the house. "And two more if Johnson doesn't shut up. My wife and children are here."

Muldoon picked out the coin, his stiff smile twitching at one corner. "I understand perfectly." He dismounted and followed Poke to the barn.

"Been here long?" Muldoon inquired while Poke pulled the harness off the pegs.

"Born here." Poke worked with the efficiency of one with long practice, fitting the collars and tightening the buckles on the matched workhorses.

"You must know everyone around." Muldoon said casually.

"Yup."

"Even the Boy Stage Robber?"

Poke paused for a moment: the memory of Sett standing right there yesterday as if he could see him if he turned and looked, the rough angry Sett with so much life happening between the years.

"No, I never met no boy stage robbers."

Muldoon stared at him flatly. Poke returned to his harnessing, the sudden need to finish this job and send Johnson and this man down the road brought up short by the realization that they were on their way to the homestead, and knew Sett Foster was there.

The edge of the sunlight crept into the canyon and warmed the side of the tent with a yellow glow. Ria woke with Sett's first stirrings, but lay still. He pulled his arm from under her head as quietly as he could, then sat up and groped for his clothes. Coy stood and stretched at the end of the tent and the man opened the tent flap so she could go out.

Ria breathed softly. She did not want to draw his attention, to let him know she was watching him through her lashes as he shook out his pants. He was close, with his back to her and there was fine golden hair on his

forearms and a swirl of it on the small of his back. She
examined the shades of his skin, the dark brown on his
forearms, the pale gold of his back and the whiteness of
his legs. She wondered if all yellow-haired Americans
had this strange variation. She had never noticed it on
Augie.

Not that she had much opportunity. Augie firmly believed that it was not healthy to expose one's bare skin
to the elements. If at all possible, he wore his union suit.
Ria did not understand it, but it was not her place to
ask. She did not even have the language at first, when
Augie would yell in his ugly American words and she
would guess at what he wanted, to avoid a whack with
a stick or a kick from his hobnailed boots.

Sett Foster ducked and stood up outside the tent. His
long legs were framed in the triangle door. She watched
him pull on the jeans and slip on the moccasins. She
closed her eyes quickly when he leaned over and stuck
his head back into the tent, gathering up the sopping
poncho and leggins and taking them with him. She heard
him drape the wet clothes over a tree limb, uncover the
dry wood and blow on the fire, and she was afraid to
move.

It was like he had forgotten she was there, but how
could he have forgotten that she was in his bed? Ria
pursed her lips. Americans were strange. How could
they be so different? She tried to remember LaBlanc,
who she supposed was her sire, although Sweetgrass
Woman had never said. He was one of the people to her.
Augie was the first American she had known, and other
than that old trapper in the bear hat who came to drink,
her only example of a white man.

Ria peeked out of the tent. Sett Foster was setting a
coffeepot of water on the fire, then he turned and gath-

ered up a pole and line. Without a backward glance at the tent, he headed toward the creek.

Ria sighed and snuggled down into the warmth of the blankets for a moment longer. She would get up and start breakfast. Even if this American was going to ignore her in his bed, he would want to eat. She stared up at the peak of the tent. She was oddly disturbed by Sett's reaction, but she could not name why. The image of his legs in the tent opening and the scent of him that still lingered on the blankets caused her thoughts to drift back to the darkness of First Wife's lodge, when she had slept in a pile with her half-sister and little brother and fallen asleep to the murmurs and sighs of her mother sharing LaBlanc's bed.

It was not like that with Augie. From the moment she had been left with him, it was clear that he would not whisper to her and stroke her hair. Instead he hollered at her in the strange tongue and gestured wildly as she tried to load his purchases into the unfamiliar wagon. They drove out onto the prairie, away from the sight of the rendezvous and the last of her people. With dark approaching, Augie pulled up in a small grove of trees and Ria scrambled down off her perch on the hides in the back of the wagon. She stood, unsure of what to do.

"Build a fire. A fire." Augie pointed to the ground. Ria responded with her mixture of French and Blackfeet.

"Fire! Fire, you little idiot!" Augie threw a stick of wood at her. Ria dodged, scooping up the stick from the ground and cocking her arm to return the missile. Her eyes glittered with anger. Then she turned her back on her irate new husband and began to gather kindling. She would have to learn his words as quickly as she could, but in the meantime she would just do what she thought should be done and watch out for the blows.

Augie had quieted down when he tasted the stew. He lounged back against the wagon wheel and watched her clean up the tin plates and lay wood on the fire. The oversize poncho hung down over her wrists and the yellow paint on her face was smudged. The long braids swung over her shoulders and the dust under her eyes made them seem too large for her.

Augie stared at the beaded design on the front of the poncho. He grumbled to himself. There was no sign of breasts, especially under the shapeless poncho. Ross said she was young, barely a woman. Or had he said almost a woman? Augie could not remember. The mountain man spoke with a thick accent and provided watered-down whiskey. Augie decided to find out what he'd paid those lousy pelts for.

The girl straightened up and sat back on her knees. She glanced over at the man across the fire, startled to find him looking right at her.

"Take off the dress," he said in his gibberish American.

"What?" she asked back in French. She reached for the coffeepot, but his harsh word and slashing motion halted her.

"The dress. Take it off." Augie leaned across the fireplace and grabbed a handful of the poncho. He pulled it up against her chin. Ria tried to shake him loose, but he dragged her nearer to him.

"This. Take it off!" He shouted into her face. She nodded and pulled back, twisting her back to him as she lifted the heavy beaded leather over her head. She carefully folded the garment and set it to the side. Then, with eyes averted, she turned back to her husband. Augie scowled at her thin body, the bones of the shoulders poking out at angles and the dark nipples the only thing womanly about her. He grunted, then pointed to her leggings.

"That too."

Ria stood and peeled off the leggings. She shivered a bit in the early evening wind. It sighed around her, the only sound as her wealthy American farmer stared at her in dismay. Tears threatened behind her downcast eyes. She was a wife, and he was obviously displeased with her. She took one deep breath, a sob barely under control. The dark edge of camp beckoned her and she thought to grab up her clothes and race into its comforting shelter before anything worse could happen, but before she could move Augie commanded, "Come here." He beckoned with his forefinger, an unmistakable gesture. She took two long steps and stood beside his seated form.

Without a word, he placed one beefy hand on her hip, the thick fingers nearly encompassing her body. Then with the other he probed between her legs, the rough calluses on his finger scraping at the tender place until she squirmed.

"Well, at least he didn't lie about you being a virgin," Augie said. Ria started to say something in her soft Blackfeet, something with a cry in the back of it.

"Shut up. I'll show you what to do." The man dragged her down beside him.

Ria closed her eyes against the memory. In the pale light of the tent, she willed the image of Augie away, and sat up to find some clothing, so that she could go fix breakfast for Sett Foster, the outlaw.

The noisy stream was gushing over the rocks and roots in its course. Sett squatted on the bank and threaded a worm on his hook. The water flowed on the south side

of the large cottonwood now, but the shape of his favorite fishing hole was mirrored under its base just as it
was when he was a boy. He dropped the line into the
water, letting the bait drift casually with the current. For
a moment he thought about the fish, the silent silver
forms dappled against the pebbles of the creek bed. He
envied them, so contained in their lives. Then the specter
of five-year-old Elizabeth peered over his shoulder, asking *Whatcha doing?* He started as if she were really
there, and sighed when he realized she was not. Her
question hung in the air, and he stared down into the
clear rushing water and answered her out loud.

"I'm hiding from that breed girl."

That the girl was in his bed right now remained a
weight upon his mind. He recalled the innocence of her
tiny form curled up against the rough wool blanket. She
knew what to do, she said, but he did not want to believe
it.

Yet, he wanted to find out.

And again, he didn't.

Sett watched the impaled worm bounce along the
gravelly bottom of the creek. Suddenly a shadow darted
out and there was a tugging on the line. Sett flipped the
trout onto the bank and whacked its head with his knife
handle.

Maybe she knew what to do, but he sure didn't.

SEVEN

Ria had the fire going and coffee water boiling when Sett came up from the creek with the string of trout. He waded through the wet grass of the clearing, stopping to greet the big mare when she lifted her head and nickered. He was wearing his jeans and moccasins, and an old woolen vest without his shirt, because she had that.

Ria combed out her hair, letting it hang loose, and belted Sett's shirt and rolled up the sleeves. She sneaked glances at the man while measuring coffee into the boiling water, then removed it from the heat to brew.

Sett was stroking the mare's face, rubbing his hands over her eyes and down the long bones to her soft muzzle. Coy trotted up from the creek bank, and went to the man and the horse as if they were old friends. Sett rubbed her ears too, and the horse snorted. Then Sett noticed Ria watching him.

"I won over your dog," he said as he made his way into the camp and handed her the string of fish. Ria took them and began to heat the frying pan.

"Coy does not like anyone."

Sett grinned down at her. "And you?" he teased.

Ria flushed. She busied herself with the trout, spreading a finger full of greens in each cleaned cavity and flopping them in the bag of flour before laying them gently in the hot greased skillet. Here in the bright sunlight last night's disgrace seemed far away. To be locked out of her own home, to lose her possessions—Ria watched the sizzling fish and was silent.

She poured coffee and handed Sett his tin cup. The peace dissolved from his face.

"This Augie Johnson will be here this afternoon. I have some questions to ask him about my family. I need to know just what you are to him, what to expect." Sett sat on the log and looked straight at her. His hazel eyes followed her face as she carefully turned the fish with a green twig. When she finally looked up, he was still trying to meet her eyes.

"What do you know?" Ria asked.

Sett blinked.

"Not very damn much. Just that everyone agrees that he's not going to be welcoming." Sett balanced the coffee on the bench. "Point is, you know a lot more about me than I know about you. And maybe you know what happened here." Sett leaned forward and ran his fingers through her hair, ending with a tug.

"I know nothing." Ria turned away from him to check the frying pan. She moved it from the flame.

"You knew there were five graves." Sett plucked one of the trout from the pan and tasted it. "This is good, this green stuff. What is it?" He finished that trout and took another.

"It's, uh, green round leaf, and nettle, purple nettle." She frowned trying to remember the name.

"Where did you learn that?"

"My mother, Sweetgrass Woman, showed me."

"Where is she now?" Sett helped himself to another.

"She went to the Sawtooth Mountains with her new husband. I came here, with Augie." Ria finally took the last fish and nibbled at it.

"Why was that?"

Ria sat back and scowled at Sett. There he was chewing away on breakfast like an innocent child while he asked her trick questions.

"We lived with LaBlanc and First Wife and my sister, on the wide river. I tend the lodge when my brother was born. That winter LaBlanc did not come home from his trap line. We wait all that summer and the next winter we were very hungry. LaBlanc did not return. My mother takes us to the big gathering of trappers, and then I came here with Augie. I have been here three winters." Ria hoped the explanation would satisfy him. Sett silently added up the winters.

"Then you were very young." Sett leaned over and poured another cup of coffee. He wished he had a better feeling about this man he had yet to meet. No one had said much about him. It was what wasn't said that bothered him. And Ria, who knew the man the best, would only say that her dog didn't like him. Sett decided he probably agreed with the dog.

Ria picked up the frying pan and looked Sett in the eyes. "I came here as wife. Augie had many nice things in his cabin. I am rich," she paused, "until Ma'am and Carolyn come. But I am First Wife, and that house is mine. They cannot lock me out. " Ria started scraping at the pan, attacking the stuck residue with a vengeance.

Sett watched her, her lips pursed and small hands gripping the frying pan so hard that the knuckles turned white.

"Augie lied to you," he said. She did not pause. "American law only allows one wife."

"I was first."

"No, you are not. He has no right to keep you here. He lied to you and is just using you like a slave."

The girl tried to blink back tears. She did not want to think about Augie and his other wife. She did not want to admit that this stranger was right. "This is my home," she said.

"It used to be my home too, but not anymore." Sett noticed the raw skin on her fingers. It must sting like hell in the hot water. He reached over and took the pan out of her hands. "You should go away, go back to your people. American law only allows one wife, and no slaves. You are too young to spend your life like this."

Ria wished he would stop. She knew he spoke the truth. It twisted in her heart, but there was no changing the fact that Ma'am was right. She was not First Wife. She owned nothing. She did not even know how to get over the mountains to the land of her grandfather.

"You will show me the way over the mountains?"

"No, I can't. I have to stay." Now the girl looked up at him, waiting for an explanation like everyone else. "Someone murdered my family."

A distant expression crossed his face. He was suddenly lost in thought, as if she were not sitting at his fire. She watched his brow wrinkle and the eyes grow dark, the calm face of the fisherman replaced with the brooding one. Suddenly, Ria remembered her mother's stories, the ones about her Grandfather Talking Crow dressing for the warpath, and the scalp raids on white men's wagons. A tingle ran up her spine.

"My grandfather killed them?" she asked.

"Your grandfather? No. White men, thieves." Sett

sighed and rubbed his hand over his brow. He turned to look Ria in the eyes. "So you really don't know what happened? You don't know if Augie knows?"

Ria tried to recall Augie saying anything to her about coming to the homestead. There was nothing. It was not like he talked to her, or asked her questions. He told her to have food ready. He told her to feed the mules, or come to his bed, or that there was a hole in his moccasins, but he did not tell her about his past. He spent the days prospecting, she thought. He carried a shovel and a pick on the mule.

Ria bit her lip. "He is looking for gold. He said once when he had been drinking whiskey that when he found gold, we would leave. He never found any." Sett got up and walked out into the sun-bright clearing. The day was warming up, the moisture on the grass misting and the gray jays in the trees squabbling raucously. Suddenly he was very tired. Last night he lay awake thinking about murders, and the night before about five unexplained graves. Now he had to think some more, about August Johnson and years and gold, but he was just too tired.

He admired the mare as she cropped eagerly at the fresh growth of spring. He could get on her right now and ride away, go someplace and sleep without dreams. There was nothing for him here, nothing but questions.

Sett rubbed his eyes with the back of his hand. He was too tired to think about it. He did not want to know any more right now. Saddling up the mare and leaving was an appealing prospect. He turned to get his saddle and nearly tripped over Ria standing behind him. She put her hands up in surprise, then placed them on his chest.

Looking up into his eyes, she saw the exhaustion on

the handsome face, and wondered what he was thinking. Whatever it was, it hurt. And he was tired. Tired and alone.

That Ria understood.

The flap of the tent was open, and sunlight streamed in, but Sett was oblivious to it. He slept soundly, only the brief wrinkling of his brow indicating the visitations in his sleep. Ria sat outside, watching him and watching the perimeter of the clearing. She waited for movement, noted each bird in the spring buds of the willows and each slow, graceful step of the mare as she grazed in the meadow. Coy had curled up in the sunshine at the edge of the canvas, and the quiet of the mountain meadow led Ria into her own thoughts as deeply as it led the man in the tent into his dreams.

So lost in daydreams was she that Coy had to give a little whine to attract her attention. The dog had risen from her sleeping place and was staring, ears pricked down the canyon. The mare also raised her head and nickered softly. Ria shook Sett's shoulder gently.

"Sett, someone's coming," she whispered as he pulled himself from the too-short nap. He rolled over and found the rifle.

"Get down." Sett motioned to the end of the tent and Ria crawled away from the door. Coy started to growl, her body tense and her tail straight out behind her. The brush crackled. Only one, Sett thought, a lone rider. He chambered a round.

"Hello the camp!" The voice was calm, familiar. "Sett, it's me, Poke!" Sett raised up from his prone position and called back.

" 'Lo, Poke, come on in. I won't shoot you now." As Sett put the rifle back alongside the bedroll, Poke

Miller rode into the meadow on his roan gelding. Sett stood up outside the tent and stretched, then went to shake his friend's hand.

"Makin' use of the tarpaulin, I see." Poke nodded toward the tent in the aspens.

"Yup. Yup. It's come in very handy." He seemed almost cheerful, Poke thought. Yesterday when they had said good-bye at the river, Poke had been genuinely worried about Sett's state of mind, and Abby had been too. The news about Rose and Elizabeth had been a lot to throw at a man.

Poke looked around the old camp. There was a coffee tin by the cold fire and clothes drying on the wild roses by the creek. Poke squinted at the clothes. An uncomfortable feeling that he was being stared at came over him. Sett was still grinning, saying nothing. Then Poke noticed the blue bitch lying in front of the tent.

"Where'd you get the dog?" he asked with a nod.

"Oh, I got more than the dog." Sett nodded toward the tent. Poke waited, but nothing happened. Sett walked over to the flap and squatted down to peer inside. Ria was huddled at the end of the bed, arms around her knees.

"Come on out," he whispered at her, "it's just my friend." Ria's eyes were big. She shook her head. "He's my friend. He's not going to hurt you." Sett reached in and grabbed her good hand. This girl was like some shy doe, so long in the mountains that she was afraid of anyone new. Sett pulled her to the door and out into the sunlight.

Poke did his best to hide his surprise. The girl was handsome, long wispy hair framing her small face and large eyes. She was wearing Sett's shirt, her bare legs stretching to the beaded moccasins.

He also recognized her. She was the breed girl that August Johnson kept.

She stared straight at him with that expressionless face that Indian women seemed to practice, eyes on his without moving. She would prefer he didn't see her, but if he was going to look, she would look back.

Sett turned from the silent girl and said to his friend, "This is Ria."

Poke reached up to touch the brim of his hat. "Nice to meet you, miss," he said and nodded. A flicker of surprise crossed Ria's face. Poke mentally added the girl to the list he was carrying in his head and spoke to Sett low-voiced.

"Sett, we got to talk. It's important."

"Should I be packing?" Sett leaned back against the log as if he hadn't a care in the world.

"Maybe. But you probably won't." Poke glanced at Ria, still standing stone-faced by Sett. "Augie Johnson just came by the post, heavy wagon, so I figure he'll be pulling into the homestead soon. He's got a man with him, tallish dandy type, but wearing his pistol in a professional way."

Sett looked at Ria questioningly.

She shrugged.

Sett persisted. "Have you ever seen a man like this? Has he been here before?"

"No."

Poke looked worried. "Sett, he already knows you're here."

"Who cares if I'm here? The laws on abandoned homesteads are pretty clear. I can't take the ranch. I do want some answers." Sett stood up from his seat on the log and paced a quick circuit in the mud around the fire pit. "Ria says that Johnson was here four years ago. He might know something."

Poke watched his friend stomp back and forth. He wanted to believe that the only reason Sett was here was to find his family, but he was sure that August Johnson would not.

"Sett, there's a lot of reasons why Johnson cares that you're here. Look around. Does this look like a successful ranch to you? Just what do you think this character is doing up here? He's not going to just sit back and let you ride off with the prize after all this work. This Johnson is a strange man. He showed up from nowhere claiming he was homesteading your old place. Then he comes through with this little girl. Not long ago he shows up with two more women and now with a gunslinger sidekick. He thinks he's got something, Sett, and he's not going to let you take it away."

Sett stopped pacing and glared.

"Poke, you are babbling," he said through gritted teeth.

"No, Sett, I'm just trying to tell you. There is more to this than you are paying attention to. I think Johnson is searching for the gold. He, and everyone else around here, is gonna think you come back for it. There's plenty of folks thought you should have hung with the rest of them. You are not safe."

Sett watched the man facing him across the campfire. He remembered being questioned by the other inmates about the missing gold, but he could tell them nothing about it. He wasn't even sure if Whitey took the money after the shoot-out with the stage driver. He had been up in the brush, holding the ready horses, when he heard the shots. According to Whitey's plan, the ambush was in the most remote of areas. They would have a day's head start on any posse, time to swing back by the line cabin and pick up the extra horses and supplies, before beginning the flight across the mountains.

The line cabin. Sett had huddled on a cot at the back of the tiny shelter while Jed cooked up bacon and fry bread and the Tejano argued with Whitey about the shooting. He could not remember much, just the angry hushed voices and the cramping in his stomach. He had never thought about the gold, never worried about where it was or if it even was. Obviously, he was alone in that.

"OK, Poke, about the gold. About me coming back for the gold. Do you believe that?" Sett said slowly.

"I don't know. I don't know if it matters." Poke shifted his feet and shook his head. "You're still my friend."

The blond man stood silently for a moment, then he turned to Ria.

"Get your stuff together. You're going back to the trading post with Poke. You'll be safer there. Poke, we got more to talk about."

Poke followed him as he headed toward the creek.

EIGHT

The cabin sat silently above the spring as the wagon cleared the trees. The door was closed and no smoke came out of the chimney. Muldoon glanced questioningly at Augie. The burly driver only scowled. Here it was mid-afternoon and no one appeared to be about. Augie had not said much about the situation, but Muldoon could add two and two or, more reasonable, two respectable women and one purchased squaw. Muldoon slowed his horse to let the wagon lead into the yard, keeping his eyes open. A cabin with three people in it should show signs of life.

Muldoon took in the dirt yard, the corral and the large barn. There was a freshly dug garden plot and a woodpile with a hatchet lopped into a stump. It looked much the same as he remembered, only more shabby. Augie Johnson certainly hadn't spent any energy fixing up the place.

The mules headed for the corral rail and stopped. Augie stayed in the seat, looking warily at the house. Where were Connie and Carolyn? Where was that lazy girl?

She should be here waiting to help him unload and feed the mules. This wasn't going to look good to the captain, all his women disappearing. Augie heaved a sigh and climbed down from the wagon seat.

The shutters over the single window opened partway and Constance called out.

"August, who's that with you?" Her voice quavered slightly.

"Connie? What's going on here? Come on out and meet my old captain," Augie bellowed at her. Muldoon flinched at the identification. The cabin door swung out and a large woman wrapped in a blanket and followed by a younger one stepped out into the yard. Augie marched up to them.

"What's going on? Where's the girl?" he demanded. The women looked at each other and then both started talking at once.

"She ran off . . ."

"Stranger sneaked up, about scared us to death . . ."

"No wood, so we locked her out . . ."

". . . said he's waiting for you."

Augie held up his hand to silence them. "Whoa. Whoa. The girl's gone? When?"

"Yesterday. She was gone all day. Didn't do her chores," Constance said. Carolyn nodded in agreement. "She ran off with this wild man. He sneaked up on us in the yard."

"We've been here a whole day alone!" Carolyn interjected.

Augie stared at the women. How could he have brought them here? Where was his mind? He couldn't stand them the first time, but he'd signed up for a second hitch. One whole day alone! They had no idea.

Augie sighed again. His wife and daughter stood in

front of him, Connie wrapped in her blanket and Carolyn hovering close to her. Augie looked over at Captain Muldoon, still sitting on his horse by the wagon. There was a slight sneer on the pale man's face as he watched the scene.

Old Augie sure had invited himself into a pickle, the captain thought. These two couldn't build a fire and the squaw that Augie had bragged on had run off with a cowboy. Muldoon waited patiently for whatever bumbling August Johnson would do next.

"Well, they couldn't have gone far. What way did they head?" Augie asked the women.

"The man said he would camp down by some pond. He wanted to talk to you. He's probably still there. He didn't sound like he would go away." Constance said.

Augie's face reddened with anger. "You mean he took the girl and didn't even have the sense to leave!" he blustered. This cowboy was pretty brash, to steal a squaw and then stick around to rub his nose in it. Augie stalked back to the wagon, jerking the pins out of the tailgate. "Come on, Cap'n, let's get this unloaded and go retrieve my property," he growled.

Muldoon sat on the horse with his hands crossed on the saddle horn, watching the big man toss supplies out of the wagon. He finally stepped off, hitched the reins to the fence and walked over to the women.

"Ma'am, Miss," he said and acknowledged them with a nod, "I am R. J. Muldoon. Are you both well after your frightening night alone?" Constance wondered if he were mocking them, but Carolyn beamed and fluttered her hands.

"Oh, thank you for your concern, Captain Muldoon," she gushed, but before she could go on Muldoon asked,

"This 'wild man' who came into the yard, did he tell you a name?"

Augie paused in his frantic unloading.

"Why, yes. He claimed this was his ranch and he was looking for his family. He called himself Foster, Sett Foster."

Muldoon swallowed grimly. His eyes narrowed under the natty bowler. Augie could go off on a tangent over the runaway girl, but if she were with Sett Foster, he'd better go prepared. The Boy Stage Robber was no longer a boy, and ten years in prison was not likely to raise a pacifist. Muldoon fingered the butt of the pistol under his coat absentmindedly. He had been surprised when Augie said that Foster had never shown up at the homestead. Now it appeared he was finally here, and there could only be one reason for it.

Ria had done everything Sett asked silently, but when Poke mounted and Sett turned to her to hand her up, she stopped him.

"Augie has a rifle and a knife he carries on his belt. Other knife in boot, this one." She pointed at her own left foot. Sett nodded. He put his hands on her belted waist to lift her onto the horse, but the girl twirled out of his grasp and extended her arm up to the mounted man. She had to hop to get her foot in the stirrup, but she swung up behind Poke with almost as much ease as she had on the big bay mare only yesterday morning.

Sett watched Ria's long braid swinging across her back as the horse disappeared into the trees. It gave him a funny feeling, like he had forgotten something, but he couldn't imagine what it was. Sett caught himself gazing into the trees long after the pair had vanished in the tangle of pale trunks.

The mare was staring after the other horse and the dog too. Sett slipped the bridle over her ears and swept off her back with his hand. Once he had saddled her, he crawled into the tent and gathered one blanket, his moccasins and saddlebags, but he left the coffee tin and fry pan next to the fire. He had curbed his first impulse—of riding into the cabin yard—with the memory of how easily Ria had held the rifle on him. His own father had chosen the easily defended site of the homestead. Sett thought he would rather be looking out than looked on from there.

He led the big horse down to the creek bank, and let her drink, then mounted and splashed past the trout weir. Just down the canyon, a trail angled up the dark hillside. Sett was surprised at how little the land had changed in fourteen years. The mossy boulders and huge trees on the north face of the mountain had never been Sett's favorite part of the homestead. He preferred the more open sage-and-cottonwood range that got some sun. Still he knew the forested land as well as he did the rest of the Cottonwoods, this area near the cabin especially.

The trail hairpinned around an outcropping of boulders, an old pine leaning out horizontal over the slope. It looked the same as it had when his younger brother, Ben, had climbed straight from the saddle, leaving no footprints, and hid in its thick branches during a game of posse and outlaws. Young Sett had ridden by the tree three times searching for him, tracking Ben's pony down off the ridge and all the way home before realizing that his brother had skinned off and sent the little horse on alone. Sett could almost smile at the memory. He would have never found his freckle-faced little brother if Ben hadn't started giggling.

He pushed the horse on up the slope. The trees made

excellent coverage, but he wanted to see the camp. As the trail broke into the park on the ridge, Sett turned and skirted the forest. Circling around the grassy clearing, he maneuvered through some rocks to a knob at the promontory of the ridge. Tying the mare securely below, he crawled up and lay in the rocks. He removed his hat and poked his head up to survey the landscape.

The rocky point was directly across the canyon from the cemetery knoll, the slanting afternoon sun bathing it in light. Sett could make out the row of gray headboards against the green grass. Up canyon the trees had grown to block the view of the cabin and barnyard, but he could see a short distance of the wagon track below it and a few views of the creek-side trail. Downstream the sage and grass of the plain rippled along to the valley floor.

There was the speck of a horse, moving fast, halfway across the trail to Miller's Post. Poke had a heat on about delivering the girl to the safety of the post, then he would be headed back, Sett was sure. He'd hoped Poke would wait until morning, but from the speed at which he was moving, he guessed Poke's decision. Sett leaned forward more and peered down into the deep pocket of canyon. There was his tent, partly hidden by the white trees, and the abandoned fire pit with the tin propped on a rock. He could have been out fishing, or hunting, it all waiting for him to walk back in, or for someone else to walk in. Sett shifted where a pebble was jabbing him in the knee. He settled in to wait. There were men coming in, and he wanted to know more about them.

Ria again sat behind a man on a horse, only this time her hands met easily in front as she clasped around him. Poke Miller was a solid presence, but his difference from Sett was most astonishing. His balance on the roan was more studied. She sat silently as the horse made his way out to the wagon tracks, then down the canyon toward the crossing. It did not occur to her to talk to Poke. She was accustomed to quiet. Coy trotted along behind with an occasional look up at the girl.

The man stirred uncomfortably in the tight grasp of the quiet breed girl. He wished he'd sent her on alone, but Sett had insisted.

Poke finally cleared his throat and attempted conversation.

"I've known Sett since we were four years old. He'll be OK."

"No," Ria answered while examining the sky. Poke flinched. When it came to knowing Sett Foster the man, the boy who grew up in prison, she had as much claim as he, maybe more.

Sett going alone to meet Augie Johnson and his well-armed companion nagged at Poke. Even with the warning—and this time Poke felt that Sett actually believed the danger possible—Sett seemed sure that he could deal with Augie. He had listened to Poke's theories about the gold, heard about the vigilante mentality of the residents of Helena and Verdy and even acknowledged that Ria being with him would tweak old Johnson's nose right when he was already angry, but he stubbornly insisted that Augie Johnson knew something about the murders. "They're my family, Poke, my mother and little sister. I got to know," he had repeated.

"And what are you going to do if you find out? Take off on a wild goose chase after renegades that were probably hanged years ago?" Poke had flapped his arms in exasperation. "Sett, you don't have many friends in these parts. The old-timers remember the Kennady gang and the new settlers are all out to clean up the country.

Remember that old Indian, Two Rivers? He turned up with a nice horse and the vigilantes accused him of stealing it, even though it was a gift from his son. They chased him clear to Canada. Would have hanged him if they caught him. They'll do the same to you, especially if Johnson cries about you stealing his Indian girl and scaring his women. It won't take much to convince folks that you are dangerous.''

Sett had stood silently throughout Poke's impassioned speech, his eyes never leaving his friend's face. ''You couldn't make yourself tell me what all happened to Elizabeth,'' he said in a low voice, ''but I got a good imagination. If folks think me dangerous, they're wise.''

Poke furrowed his brow as he rode along with the breed girl. She said no more, but watched the terrain as the trail dipped down into the crossing. The sun was angling toward the Rockies, late afternoon but with the long twilight of summer still left in the day. Poke made a decision. He would take Ria to the post, collect his ammunition and head back. It was Sett's family, as close to his own as was possible. If there was avenging to be done, he would be in on it.

Suddenly Ria turned and let out a little cry.

''Stop. Stop.''

Poke reined up the roan and dropped his hand to the rifle butt.

''What's wrong?'' He peered back down the trail, expecting to see a rider following.

''Coy is gone,'' the girl said, ''I must go back.''

''Oh, she's probably just digging after some gopher.'' Poke started to turn the horse back toward the trading post, but the girl squirmed down off the broad rump.

''No, she does not leave me. Something is wrong,''

Ria insisted. Poke rode alongside her and grabbed her sleeve.

"Look, the dog will be OK. Sett wants you safe at the post. We don't have time to waste. Now, get up here." He hauled the unwilling girl back onto the horse. She sat sullen behind him, hands at her sides. He kicked the horse on down the track.

The trail dipped down into the crossing; the spring waters rushing from the previous night's rain splashed over the roan's knees, and Poke urged him into the swollen stream. The footing was slick, and as the horse slid on the rocks Poke felt the breed girl's strong fingers on his upper arm, then he was neatly flipped to the off side, landing in breathtaking, icy water.

The startled roan lunged forward, and Ria clung to the saddle to stay on. Poke scrambled for his footing. She pulled herself into the saddle and spun the horse around. She looked him straight in the eye, like the Indian women do. Then she stole his horse and headed back up the canyon. Poke yelled after her.

"Hey! Damn you! Get back here!"

It would be a long walk on to the post.

The late afternoon sun warmed his shoulders and Sett leaned back against the rocks. He mentally traced Augie Johnson's journey in a heavily laden wagon compared to Poke's swift mounted one, their discussion and his ride up the hill. He thought it would be a while yet. Augie didn't seem to have extra saddle horses, so he'd have to unhitch a mule. Still no point in being caught asleep. Sett listened for the mare, then glanced back down at the valley floor. Poke and Ria were out of sight, swallowed by the haze. The expanse was deafening, so silent but for the chewing of the mare tied below and the arguing of the blue jays in the pines.

He had always liked the high places, as a boy climbing every peak and knob around the cabin. He had even sat on this one before, although it was not his favorite view. That was reserved for the line cabin, sitting up under the divide at the prolific headwaters of the creek. He had often thought of homesteading that tract adjoining his family's, even though it was about as high as anyone would think of ranching. It would be a long pull in winter, but he wondered if the daily sight of range after range, mountain after mountain, might not be worth it.

The vision had sustained him in the dark cell of the prison, the reaching memory of earth and sky meeting somewhere yonder. In the winter, confined for days inside the stone walls, Sett had not seen the sky at all. But on the first clear days when the prisoners were marched out to cut wood, he had found himself mesmerized by it, gazing up to the point of stumbling over his shackles. Since his release he had never minded sleeping outside, his last memory at night the black dome of sky and his first sight at waking the sunrise. Sitting up here on the rocky knob, even knowing about his family did not stop his pleasure at being able to look into the distance.

A faint noise from up canyon brought his attention to the patch of trail he could see between the trees. Two riders, one a hefty man on a mule wearing a floppy hat, the other tall and thin and wearing a long coat unbuttoned in the afternoon heat, disappeared from his sight behind the thick growth, reappearing again in the next clearing. They were coming in quietly, walking their mounts and speaking lowly or not at all.

The next time the riders went behind the trees, Sett

rolled cautiously to get a better view of his camp. The little meadow glimmered in the sun, the stream falling cheerfully. He wondered where the men were, wondered if they had for some reason ridden past, when he saw a movement at the edge of the cottonwoods. Augie Johnson's sagging hat was below, hesitating before entering the meadow. It bobbed and paused as Augie scanned the camp for a sign of the Foster boy and his runaway breed girl. Finally he rode into the open, calling in a booming voice, "Hello! Hello!" He paused in the middle of the clearing, turning the mule slowly as he looked for Sett. He sat there confusedly like some sort of bait, Sett thought.

Sett searched the trees for the other man. Where was he? Sett raised his head enough to see his mare on her tether under the ridge. She gazed up at Sett, her big ears swiveling.

In the meadow, Augie dismounted and walked into the camp, poking at the cold fire with his boot toe and peering into the tent. He waded through the footprints around the fire pit. Finally, he looked up the canyon and shrugged.

"No one here," he called out. There was no response, so he hollered louder, "No one here, Cap'n!" Sett followed the heavy man's gaze and there, hidden by the boulders of the creek, was the chestnut horse. The man called Captain stood up from his prone position among the rocks and slapped his hat back on his head.

"Shut up, you blithering fool," he snarled. Each word drifted up to Sett in the still mountain air. Line of sight, Sett's father had reminded him. Step over the ridge and you could yell for help for hours and no one could hear, but if they can see you, they can hear you. Sett barely breathed. The captain caught up his horse and led him into the clearing to confront his noisy ally.

"Johnson, if you do everything with this much foresight, it's no wonder you haven't found the cache," Muldoon growled as he stalked into the camp. Augie had the decency to look chastened. Muldoon glanced around at the coffee tin by the fire and the bedding in the tent.

"This Boy Robber is probably sitting up there somewhere laughing at us. He didn't leave for good." Muldoon scanned the ridges above the camp.

Sett held his breath as the thin man's sharp eyes skimmed over the rocky knoll without pause. The chestnut stud was not so easily fooled. He pricked his ears up toward the ridge and widened his nostrils. Sett glanced with alarm at his big mare. She was also staring intently, even though she was safely out of sight beyond the bank. The scent of the other horse held her interest. It would only be a matter of moments before one neighed to the other. *Damn*, Sett thought, *just my luck that this Captain guy is riding a stud horse.*

The men in the camp were absorbed in other matters. Augie kicked at the coffee tin. "He's got my squaw. I want her back. I paid good money for her and I'm not goin' to just give her away," he complained. Muldoon crossed his arms.

"It ever occur to you that this Foster kid could be our ticket to finding that gold? He knows where it is if anyone does. Get your mind off your dick for a few moments and think. Besides that, he could be sitting somewhere with a rifle laying right on one of us, right now!"

Sett smiled. He inched up until his head was clear of the rocks and the view unobstructed. Then he chambered a round in the Winchester.

The two men whirled around, searching for the source of the noise.

"You hear that?" Augie said.

"Shut up, Johnson." Muldoon finally settled on peering up in the general direction of Sett's perch in the rocks. "Foster? We come to talk with you, peaceable. There's no need to go shooting." His voice was rational and calm, but inside Muldoon was seething. Dimwitted Johnson had sprung the trap. It galled him to be caught so in sights by some unknown farm boy. Of course, the Boy Stage Robber had grown up in prison. Muldoon knew now he should have never left his hiding place in the boulders. He scrutinized the jumble of rocks, trying to make out the gunman's location.

"Foster, we just come to talk," he called again.

"That's good, 'cause I got something I want to talk about too." Sett sat up from his nest in the gravel and crawled to the edge of the cliff. Casually, as if enjoying the view, he swung his feet over the edge and cradled the rifle across his knees. Without taking his eyes from the pair below him, he placed his dusty hat back on his head. The dying evening sun slanted behind him, casting long shadows.

Muldoon had to squint against the glare to make out the silhouette. A big man, tall, with long pale hair. No boy. He could not see the face, but the body was relaxed, legs swinging slightly. Muldoon fought the urge to raise his hands in surrender; Augie actually did.

"Put your hands down, for crissakes," Muldoon hissed at him. "Stay shut up and let me handle this." He stepped forward a little and shouted up at Sett. "I'm R. J. Muldoon. Mr. Johnson here and I just rode in from town this afternoon, and got word you wanted to see us." There was no response from the man on the cliff.

"You are Foster, aren't you?" Muldoon hated not being able to see the gunman's face. The dark outline gave no clues to his disposition.

"I'm Sett Foster," the figure said with a nod, voice carefully under control.

"Why don't you come into the house for dinner? We can talk civilized like the gentlemen we are," Muldoon suggested. Sett shifted the rifle.

"Few folks would call me civilized; fewer would call me a gentleman. I'll do my talking from here." Sett watched Muldoon closely.

August Johnson was standing, hands stiff and away from his sides. He looked scared, but Muldoon looked dangerous, calm and calculating. Augie wouldn't go for his gun, but Muldoon might. Sett addressed the fat man while never taking his eyes off the other.

"When did you come here to take over the homestead?"

Augie shuffled a bit and glanced quickly at Muldoon. "I don't know, three maybe three and a half years ago. It was spring. I got here in spring."

"Really? When in spring? As I remember spring up here comes about end of May."

"Oh, early. Early spring, before the snowmelt." Augie furrowed his brow trying to follow the line of questions. Muldoon scowled at him but could not think of anything else to say but the truth.

"What was in the cabin?"

Augie squinted. The sun was in his eyes, blinding him.

"What was in the cabin? Was there anything in the cabin?" Sett tried to keep the annoyance from his voice. There was this man, peering up at him like a mole and sweating in the early chill of the mountain evening, and he was the one clue to information about his family's murders.

"Uhh, there was some things, not much. Oh, a wash-basin and pitcher and a fry pan. It had been pretty much gone through." Augie nodded his head vigorously. Sett lifted the rifle up a little with his knee.

"In the middle of winter, when the trails are nearly impassable, the cabin had been gone through?"

" 'Pears so, yes, 'pears so." Augie sighed with relief. Maybe now the intense questioning was over. He glanced again at Muldoon, remembering the *I'll take care of this*. Surely the cap'n was thinking up a way out of this.

He was.

The sun would soon drop behind the mountain, plung-ing the little meadow into darkness. Foster would lose his advantage, and Muldoon would be able to see him better than he could be seen. It was a long shot for a pistol, and uphill. His first shot would have to count, or the Boy Stage Robber would be lobbing rifle slugs at them. Still, he was sitting up there smugly, dangling his legs like a child. Like shooting a bird off a tree branch. Muldoon felt much better now that he had a plan. He kept a close eye on the descending sun.

"Keep talking," he muttered to Augie.

Augie stared down at his own nose while trying to think of something to say. He peered around the camp until his eyes lit on the canvas tent. He pulled himself up into a belligerent stance.

"Hey, where's my Injun girl?" he bellowed up at the man on the cliff. "She up there with you?"

Muldoon gave a bare shake of his head.

"No, she's not here," Sett replied.

"Well, she better get on back to the cabin," Augie

continued. "She got work to do. She got no business running off."

"Seems she doesn't agree." Sett noted the shadow cast by the setting sun. He didn't have time to fight over Ria right now. He asked, "Mr. Johnson, how'd you know the cabin was there in the middle of winter?"

The heavyset man paused for a second. "What do you mean?" he stuttered.

"I mean, even you aren't stupid enough to go prospecting in that weather. You knew the cabin was there and was empty." Sett's voice was calm, but his grip on the rifle tightened. Augie looked at his partner, who never took his eyes off the dark shape with the sun over its shoulder.

"Keep talking. We got to keep him there till the sun sets," Muldoon whispered. "You want to get your squaw back, don't you?"

Augie clenched his blocky jaw. "Yeah," he muttered. Then he yelled up at Sett, "Where's my girl? What right you got scaring my wife and stealing my property? You're nothing but a two-bit convict. Send the girl out now!"

"Ria's not here, Mr. Johnson, and slavery was abolished years ago. She left on her own, no one stole her." Sett could not help the exasperation in his voice. He wanted to know about his family, about the few possessions left to him. Ria said there were many nice things in the cabin. This talking to August Johnson was getting nowhere. The heavy man was fidgeting, looking nervously at his partner, who was still staring intently up at Sett. The sun was touching the peaks behind him, the shadow moving steadily into the canyon.

                    •   •   •

Muldoon licked his lips. He stretched his right hand, arching the fingers. The man on the cliff did not seem to notice. Sett Foster's time was about to run out.

Sett motioned with his rifle muzzle at the pair in the camp. "Look at that. See that little cemetery up there?" Off balance, Augie swiveled to look where he pointed. "That's my family. That's my father and brother, dead while I was in prison. That's my mama and my little sister, murdered, just before you moved into my home. I want to know what you know, Mr. Johnson, and I want my family's things. You look too, Captain Muldoon, case it might kindle a memory."

Muldoon turned his back to Sett, gritting his teeth. The last of the sunlight crowned the hill with its five weathered markers. Deep shadows surrounded the camp, and Muldoon smoothly drew his weapon and spun around to the rocky point. The sky was pale with dying daylight, and Sett Foster was gone.

NINE

The roan pounded up the wagon track until Poke's voice faded, then Ria slowed him to a walk. She did not want to miss a sign of her dog, even though she was certain where the blue bitch had gone. Coy had taken to the tall blond man, letting him stroke her ears and sitting at his feet.

Ria fished around with her moccasined toes for the stirrups. Poke Miller was not that much taller than her, and if she stretched, she could get purchase. The stocky roan followed her commands willingly, not seeming to care about the sudden change in riders.

It had been years since she had ridden, since the last summer with LaBlanc in the lodge on the Missouri. He had let her ride his pack horse on gathering trips with her mother. It was a carefree time, the only time like that she could remember. Sweetgrass Woman carried Ria's baby brother, in the cradleboard on the saddle. First Wife's youngest rode behind Ria on the old horse. The small group would traverse the slopes of the Rockies, seeking wild onions or skunk cabbage or salmonberries. Ria remembered a lot of laughter, loping through a meadow, her half-sister tilted off behind. Her mother told them stories of life with her grandfather, of great celebrations and dances that went on all night. Ria glanced north at mountains with their hidden passes and secret trails. If only she knew the way over the mountains.

The ridges ahead were bathed in the remaining light of the evening sun, the canyon plunged into darkness. Sett was up there somewhere—but so was Augie. The evening was chilling rapidly as the rare clear night settled around the mountains. Ria became conscious of her lack of a coat. She looked back at Miller's Post, a dark stain on the slope across the valley. She could not go there, not after stealing the horse. The girl bit her lip. Maybe Sett would be angry too.

The draft up the canyon reminded her of the more immediate problem. She needed warmer clothes. Ria sent the horse off the trail and into the brush along the creek. It would be slower going, but there would be less chance of meeting up with Augie.

Poke watched the fading figure of the horse, then splashed the clear water in exasperation. He waded over to the bank and seated himself on the nearest dry boulder. He pried off each boot and emptied the water from it, making a small puddle in the dust of the wagon trail. After a moment's consideration of the post in the distance, he worked off the woolen socks and wrung them out. Damn that girl. There was no understanding Indian women. Poke set his bare feet down on a rock and waited for them to dry in the arid mountain air. With night fast approaching, he became aware of his soaked trousers and shirt. Again he calculated the walk home.

He would get there well after dark. The temperature would drop twenty degrees or more.

Poke struggled his socks and boots back on, and began the trudge down the trail. The girl had known Sett Foster two days. Poke had known the boy for years.

Poke clearly remembered Sett's gangly elbows jabbing him as the two boys shared a pallet in the loft of the cabin. He could picture the wry smile slinking across Sett's face when his mother sent him back outside to wash his neck before dinner. That summer, that summer of the thirteenth birthdays, Poke had lived with the Fosters, helping drive the hay rake and carrying water to the vegetables and playing Outlaws and Posse with Sett and Ben and even little Elizabeth.

In early evening, after the dinner was served and the stock fed, the boys would roam out over the homestead. Two elected to be posse, and stayed to help with the dishes. "Outlaw" would leave immediately. The long Montana twilight was worth hours of seeking and hiding.

Poke marched forward at a steady pace. Already his heels were raw from the wet socks and boots. The first night at the Foster cabin, he had drawn the short straw, Outlaw. Ben had found him immediately, under the loose hay in the loft of the barn. "You're goin' to have to do better than that!" the freckle-faced ten-year-old had laughed. The next time he drew Outlaw, they sent Elizabeth with him. She had crawled, holding her nose, under the edge of the outhouse floor. There they lay until sunset, when they could claim victory and reappear at the cabin without divulging their hiding place.

It was more than a game, especially to Sett. He sought out the deepest hiding spots, and often tracked his trackers. Back in the loft of the cabin, he would kid Poke about his search up the hogback, or the lost trail at the creek. It was Sett's main interest, that and what lay over the mountains. Cattle were coming into the valley, and Sett practiced his roping and riding, much to his mother and father's dismay.

We should have seen it coming, Poke thought as he shivered in his wet clothes. The post could be seen in the twilight, the lamps shining feebly against the backdrop of the breaks. Really it was no surprise that Sett had jumped at the chance of adventure.

Poke recalled the fateful evening, when their search for Ben had led them down the canyon, only to find Ben peeking through the rocks and motioning them to be silent.

There were strangers camped at the old Blackfeet grounds, three men with six horses. The boys huddled in the boulders and eavesdropped while the white-haired man argued with the tall thin one.

"You gotta repicket the horses. Someone's gotta do it and I say you."

Poke had never seen such pale hair on a young man before. It was almost translucent, with silver eyebrows leaping up and down as he spoke. The thin man grumbled, "I catched them all this mornin', and unpacked them all tonight. When do I get to sit down and rest?"

There was a dark man sitting silently by the fire. He wore a large Texas sombrero, shaped out flat to shade his face. He gave no acknowledgment to the discussion, looking only at the flames and the fry pan of beans he stirred.

"Them horses need all the grass they can get. They're our ticket across the Tenderfoot." The pale man rested one hand on his hip, rested it near the butt of the holstered gun.

"Well, Whitey, you better find yourself a wrangler, then, 'cause I say every man should take care of his own horses!" The man sat down on the log and pulled his knife from his belt sheath. He carefully unrolled a waxed paper and cut a plug of tobacco, then fitted it into his lip without looking at his companions. The white-haired man snorted in disgust and turned to the man by the fire.

"Move them yourself, Whitey," the Tejano murmured without moving. The one they called Whitey stood for a moment, then stalked away toward the picket line.

The sun was sliding behind the ridge and Sett motioned his companions away from their hiding place in the boulders.

"We better get home before Pa comes looking for us," he suggested to his wide-eyed little brother. All the way back, Poke watched the gleam in his friend's eyes, watched the energy stir around in the lanky body and the plan form until resolve settled. *I should have known right then,* Poke thought again, as rocks jabbed through his soaked boots and the lights of his home stayed a long walk away.

"Damn!" Muldoon stared up at the line of rimrocks.

"Where'd he go?" Augie asked stupidly. Muldoon did not holster his guns. The evening was still but for settling calls of the birds and a soft dying rustle of the wind in the cottonwoods. Augie peered around, nervous from his captain's frozen stance. The chestnut stud horse nickered and pricked his ears up the canyon. Augie's mule flopped his ears forward and Muldoon turned in the same direction. There was no answer to the horse's call.

"We'd better head back to the cabin. Don't want to be out here all night."

Augie was sweating in the gathering darkness. Muldoon said nothing, peering up the narrow rise of the canyon intently.

"Maybe we should go." Augie fidgeted with his shirt buttons.

"Shush," Muldoon hissed at him. The night descended into the canyon, the sky sinking down into the pines. Behind them, along the flattening ridge, there was a crashing in the brush, then silence. Augie wheeled around. Muldoon just cocked his head. Was it Sett Foster, fleeing toward Miller's Post? Or just some animal, some elk or mule deer? The creek babbled away in the darkness and Muldoon finally slid his gun back into the holster. He caught up his horse and headed back for the homestead.

Sett watched them go. He was crouched in the thicket where the elk had been, startled when Sett waved his hat. The big mare was tied in the draw up canyon, and Sett picked his way back along the elk trail in the darkness. It had been hours since he had eaten and he considered the supplies stored away in the tent. He wouldn't get much sleep in camp, that he knew. The sky was clear and the waning moon would not provide much light. He hoped again that Poke would wait until morning to come back.

"Hooo mare," he whispered as he approached the trees. The horse blew at him, and he tightened up the girth.

They slid down the steep trail into the camp, and Sett purposely rode right up to the tent, leaving their tracks over those of Augie and his gunslinging partner. He gathered up his supplies, packing quickly in the dark.

Seems like he spent a lot of time moving away, and never quite knowing where he was headed next. He rolled the mirror and his razor and his extra shirt inside the blanket, and that inside the tarpaulin. The sack of flour, the paper rolls of dried meat and pemmican, and the johnnycakes that Samantha had packed for him went into the saddlebags, along with the moccasins and the coffee tin. The nosebag full of grain hung on the saddle horn, the rifle in the scabbard under his leg.

By the time he was mounted, the camp looked much like it had when he arrived the few days before, but for the ashes and trampled ground. He guided the mare up the canyon, then up the north ridge to avoid the cabin yard. A pale golden light from the window fell into the yard. Sett could smell the wood smoke from the stove. It made him swallow and blink. It was no longer his home.

The trail started up toward the cemetery, but at the fork he turned up the slope into the park. This time he picked his way slowly, not letting the mare fly across the grass like he had the other morning. It brought Ria to mind briefly. He would have to check on her soon at Miller's. If she was still there. Seemed she wanted to get away too.

Sett returned to the business at hand of threading his way over the mountain without leaving a trail.

Muldoon had not said a word on the ride back to the cabin. Augie followed nervously behind. The captain was not happy. And when he was unhappy, he got mean.

Constance unbarred the door as they approached. She peered behind them as if expecting to see the wild man Sett Foster following them into the yard. When the men came into the cabin, she started to close the door.

"Leave it open," Muldoon commanded. He took a seat on the far side of the table. The fresh air was welcome in the smoky cabin. He removed his hat and laid it on the bench.

Augie silently went over and examined the fire in the stove, adjusted the damper and lifted the lid of the pot. He took a long sniff, but the contents seemed to be without flavor.

"Well, what happened?" Constance stuck her hands on her hips. Carolyn stood behind her, an eager twin. "Did you find him? What did he say?"

Muldoon ignored her. Augie shook his head.

"He didn't say nothing. When's dinner?" He sat heavily. "Carolyn, get me and the cap'n a cup of coffee."

The girl didn't move. "We didn't make coffee," she said.

"No coffee? Just make some then. What you expect us to drink?" He rubbed his head with his hand. "I got to apologize for my women, Cap'n. The girl did all of the cooking."

Constance had not budged from her stance. "What do you mean he said nothing? Did you talk to him? Is he still out there? Maybe we should close the door!"

"We'll leave the door open," Muldoon said quietly. "Is there a meal or shall I get something from my saddlebags?"

Constance hesitated for a moment, eyeing this stranger who gave orders in her house, then she gathered the tin plates off the sideboard. Carolyn was watching the water in the coffeepot. She had thrown in a handful of grounds, and now was waiting for it to boil. Constance elbowed her out of the way. She ladled a scoop of boiled meat over a sad-looking biscuit and set it in front of Muldoon. Then she served August. The coffee boiled over on the back of the stove, and Carolyn dove for it but not before it doused much of the fire. Augie groaned.

Muldoon chewed thoughtfully on the stringy meat. Augie was right; his wife wasn't much of a cook. Still he forked the bland mass into his mouth and attacked the hard biscuit methodically. He stared at the doorway, not because he thought that Sett Foster would come bursting through, even though the women obviously did. The doorway led into his past.

Muldoon had killed many men, some in war and some in anger. It was not something that he dwelled on. But he had killed few women, and only one old gray-haired woman. Somehow over the years it was the one killing that remained in his dreams.

But what was he to do, old woman coming at him like that, ax raised over her head and demanding ''Leave that alone!'' He had used his rifle butt, bringing it down on the sparse-haired pate and turning back to the chest, which had held nothing but old pictures and lace. The old woman had clawed at the floorboards, her scratching growing more feeble until she was still.

That episode was a blur anyway, like the battles near the end of the war. Nine men all fired up about finding treasure and riding down into the barnyard with adrenaline and whiskey peaking in their veins. Muldoon had not controlled them, just ridden along. Then a shot was fired and the man had fallen, and another shot was fired, this one from the window of the cabin. Someone kept yelling, ''Don't burn the house!'' Someone else yelled, ''Look in the barn,'' and that was where Augie and he and Irish Joe were when Owen came in with the blond girl over his shoulder. One thing led to another.

Muldoon chewed slowly and stared out the door. It must be here. Why would they fight so hard if it were not here? They had fought as if they had something to lose.

"So what are we going to do?" Constance's whiny voice pried into his thoughts. He looked over at her but she was focusing on Augie as he attacked the biscuit with his hunting knife.

"Well, you are not going to do nothing, 'cept stay close to the house," Augie said. Carolyn stopped pushing her meat around on the plate.

"Captain Muldoon," she said, wide-eyed, "is he really dangerous? I mean, he was pretty scary sneaking up on us and all, but he said he was looking for his family. Of course, Ria didn't think he was dangerous!"

Augie glared at his daughter. Muldoon put down his fork.

"Miss, Sett Foster spent ten years in the territorial prison for robbing and murdering a stage driver. I would consider him dangerous."

"Maybe we should inform the law. Is there a sheriff in Verdy?" Carolyn asked.

"Carolyn, this is the frontier. There's no marshal closer than Helena, and that's fine," Augie said through a mouthful of biscuit.

"Well, I just don't feel comfortable here with an outlaw on the loose." Constance began clearing the table. "Maybe Carolyn and I should go into town."

"For crying out loud, Connie, there is no town around here. I don't have time to take you into Verdy."

"We could wait at Miller's Post for a freighter," the woman said resolutely.

Muldoon finished his meal and sat back to stare at the

coffeepot. No one had offered to pour and the coffee was boiling away. It would hardly be drinkable now. He cleared his throat.

"That would be a good idea. Make sure the women are safe." He caught Augie's eye, but the big man just scowled at him. Constance looked surprised, then she smiled graciously at Muldoon.

"Thank you, Captain. It's nice to know there are some gentlemen left in this world."

Samantha Miller started out of her chair at the knock on the door. For a moment she was confused, wondering why she was sleeping in the rocker by the stove and why the cabin was so dark. She fumbled her way to the solid plank door and leaned against it.

"Who's there?" she called with her hand on the brace.

"Sam, it's me. Open the door."

Samantha pulled the bar up out of its keepers, and the door swung open. Poke stood wearily leaning against the frame.

"Poke! What happened? I was so worried!" Samantha pulled him into the warm room. "You're all wet!" She ushered him closer to the stove and opened the damper. As she loaded the wood into the firebox, Poke shivered and rubbed his hands.

"Sam, I cannot believe it myself." Poke shook his head. "I found Sett, but he had that little breed girl of Johnson's with him. He wanted me to bring her back here for safekeeping while he went to meet with Johnson."

"The breed girl? What's she got to do with this?" Samantha began to unbutton his shirt, peeling the wet fabric off his skin.

"Sett has hooked up with her somehow. I guess she ran off from Johnson and Sett took her in. Anyway, the girl and I were on our way back here and, well, at the crossing, you know, the steep one on Foster Creek," Poke ran a hand through his thin hair, "she jumped me. Stole my horse."

Samantha paused "She stole Roanie?"

"Yeah."

"But you're all right?"

"Yeah," Poke said miserably. "I gotta get back there. Sett could be in trouble."

Samantha wrapped a blanket around her husband's shoulders and set about putting on the kettle for tea.

"You can't go back until morning, Poke. It's late and you would never find him in the dark." She kept her voice low so as not to wake the children or Abby, but Poke recognized the dismay. She fussed over the tea herbs and stirred the fire. "Besides, Sett Foster looks like he can take care of himself."

"Maybe. Sett thinks Johnson knows something about the murders. Ria says Johnson was there. She says he's looking for the gold and moved into the cabin right after we found Rose and Elizabeth."

"Ria?" Samantha handed Poke a steaming cup of tea.

"The girl." Poke took a sip. "I don't know if she headed back to Sett or just saw an opportunity to gain a head start on old August Johnson. She's not much older than Gail, once I saw her up close. Just a little girl."

"Big enough to toss you into the creek," Samantha said ruefully.

"Yeah, big enough." Poke thought of Sett presenting the girl there in camp. It gnawed at him that he would have to tell Sett that she had run off, that he had not fulfilled his promise to protect her. For a moment he considered going after her first, then he remembered the gunslinger.

"I didn't like the looks of that guy with Johnson. He might not be willing to just talk. Ria thought Sett could need help."

"Ria thought? Now you are going to do something like this because of what a half-breed runaway girl thought?" Samantha snapped.

"She knows Augie Johnson better than anyone. She probably knows Sett best too. I got to listen to what she says. I don't think Sett realizes how dangerous it could be."

"Sett Foster spent ten years in prison. He must know plenty about dangerous men." Samantha set her jaw and glared at her husband. That he was loyal, and generous and responsible, were good traits; it was why she loved him. Still . . . "You are leaving your family here alone and putting your life in jeopardy for the sake of a man you haven't seen since you were children."

Poke stood up and set the cup on the sideboard. Then he turned to face Samantha.

"You remember when Pa found Rose and Elizabeth. You remember what was done to them. The men who did that are still around. I am not risking my life for Sett; but I have a share in his revenge. And I have to protect my own." Poke pulled her to him, stroking her hair when he felt the tears on his bare skin. "I have to go back, Sam."

"Wait until morning. Stay here until it's light," she begged. He led her across the dark room to their bed. There were only a few hours till sunrise.

TEN

Ria dismounted and tied the roan securely in the aspens below the camp. She crept quietly along the fishing trail, the trees blocking the moonlight. She could whistle for Coy, but what if Augie was near? There was no smell of smoke, no flickering campfire, no movement from the dark clearing. Her heart pounded in her chest and her mouth felt so dry she was sure she could not whistle for her dog. Where was Sett Foster? She crawled closer. There was no sign of the camp. Ria moved down closer to the creek, stepping from stone to stone along the rushing water. There was the beaver dam, the gushing spillway below the placid pool. There was the trout weir. Ria stood still, smelling the canyon air and listening, then she walked up the bank into the deserted camp.

It was all gone. Even in the dark she could make out the bare tent frame, the blank space of the fire pit, and the trampled earth. She stared at it for only a moment before fading back into the trees.

Once back to the horse, she mounted and started up

the trail toward the cabin. Sett Foster was gone, where to she had no idea.

Ria tied the horse again in the elk park above the cabin, and slid down the wet bank for a view of the homestead. She tucked her arms inside the poncho and shivered. The quickly chilling night air seeped under the trees, and the warm glow of the lanterns in the cabin reminded her of her need.

The wagon was parked in its usual place, the supplies unloaded into the barn. She wanted her coat, or at least a blanket, and some provisions, to try for Grandfather's land over the mountains. She lay under the sheltering pines and plotted her approach.

The ground around the spring was soft and her moccasins sunk as she tiptoed across. The shadow of the barn hid her from the cabin, and she slid along the back wall with a murmur to the mules. They strained their long ears at her, hoping for some hay, but she sidled past them and vaulted over the stanchion into the barn. In the dark, she felt her way around the small stack of hay. Soon the hay in the meadows would need cutting, and she wondered if Augie would remember to do it without her. The corner was piled high with hastily unpacked supplies. Ria groped through the bundles and boxes, trying to locate by feel and smell the necessary items for her journey.

She opened the sack of dried beans, scooping handfuls into an old feed sack, then followed that with handfuls of cornmeal. She set aside the sack of flour, thinking it too heavy to carry. There were three new trade blankets and she chose two, and wrapped them up to carry a tin pan and kettle. For a moment she contemplated the pile in the dim light. One of the mules lopped his ears toward the door, and Ria froze as she heard the voices in the yard.

". . . Connie ain't much of a cook," Augie was muttering as the footsteps neared the door. Ria grabbed up her tackle and looked around wildly for a place to hide. The grain bin sat behind her in the farthest corner of the barn, its sloping lid open against the wall. It was nearly empty, and she crawled into the nest of oats and pulled the lid shut over her. The barn door squeaked and there was an unfamiliar voice.

"We got other things to worry about beside your bed wench. Why do you think Foster was asking so many questions?" Ria heard the mules slam the shelter walls in anticipation of their feed.

"He got my property and I want it back. I paid plenty for that girl and I ain't going to give her away."

"Crissakes, Johnson, think for a moment if that's not too much strain," the voice sneered. "He's suspicious. He thinks you know something." Ria breathed the dusty air of the grain bin softly. Through the splits in the boards she could see Augie's back as he forked hay over the divider to the eager mules. The stranger was out of sight, rustling around in one of the unused stalls.

"He could be a problem," the disembodied voice continued. Augie straightened from his chore.

"Cap'n, I took this place fair and square. It was abandoned."

"More than that, Johnson. He's looking for the killers." Now the man called Cap'n sounded really impatient. "Surely you remember. The man Owens shot in the yard? The women? The blond one? Hell, she was tied right there!" The thin man moved into Ria's view. He had a tight-jawed face and iron eyes and he flashed a pointed look at the tie ring in the end stall.

"You were in charge of that," Augie mumbled. He began to pitch hay again.

"Sett Foster isn't asking me any questions, but he suspects you. That was his sister. If he figures it out, he'll kill you." The man took off his long coat, revealing the walnut-handled revolver in the holster on his hips. Then he removed his vest.

"I ain't afraid of the Boy Stage Robber. Maybe I'll kill him first." Augie stabbed the pitchfork into the dwindling pile of hay. Ria held her breath, wishing beyond hope that Augie would forget to grain the mules again tonight.

He turned away. "I got a score to settle with this Foster. He took my girl, and now he's scared my women. Connie wants to leave tomorrow."

"Let 'em go." The cap'n disappeared from sight again, and Ria strained to hear where he was in the barn. "We're going to have enough to do without baby-sitting your women. Foster must know where the gold is. We got to follow him to find it."

"If I see him, I'm going to shoot him," Augie said stubbornly.

Muldoon cleared his throat. "That would be short-sighted of you, Johnson."

"That would be what he deserves after taking my girl right out of my house." Augie left Ria's sight and she blinked the fine oat dust out of her eyes. She dared not move for fear of attracting the men's interest to the grain bin. The bundle of supplies in her lap was getting heavy and her legs were cramping from holding one position. She heard Augie shuffling toward the door and then the stranger sighed and said, "Turn out the lantern when you leave, will you?"

The scene through the crack fell dark.

Ria held her breath. She could hear the mules chomping their hay and stomping the dirt floor of the shelter. In the pines just behind the barn, an owl called into the night. The moments ticked past, measured only by her shallow breathing as she strained to hear the man across the barn. Maybe he would snore, and she could tell when he was asleep. But there was no sound. A mouse ventured into the grain bin, scratching at the wood and scurrying over Ria's foot. She did not move. She measured in her mind the distance from the bin to the partial wall between the barn and the mule shelter. If she could just get over that wall, she would be into the cover of the forest and on her way back to the roan gelding tied up the slope. If she could just get over the wall.

Ria shifted a bit and leaned back against the splintery boards of the bin. She must be patient, be sure that the stranger with the gun was sound asleep, if she was to have any chance of sneaking out of the barn. She hugged her prized supplies to her chest and tried to plan where she would go after getting out of this predicament. She wondered where Sett Foster was, if he had gone to Miller's Post and discovered that she had pushed his friend into the creek and stolen the horse. How long before Miller came after her? And where was Coy? Ria closed her eyes against the irritating dust of the grain bin.

The fine bay mare picked her way out of the canyon, stepping cautiously around the silver boulders in the moonlight. The moon rose, its crescent giving Sett an eerie view of the breaks ahead. He pulled up, dismounted and took the nose bag off the saddle horn. While the mare ate her grain, he unwrapped one of the johnnycakes and stared out at the unfolding landscape.

It always surprised him, and now the space of it made

him dizzy. It was not like he had not been to the tops
of mountains during his ramblings, but this great space
drew him into it.

And he was not yet to the top. From this point at the
head of what the Blackfeet called Buffalo Canyon, the
breaks stacked up on each other like disarrayed pan-
cakes, their black rocky edges dripping dark green trees.
Each level was amazingly higher than the last, disappearing from view before the mind could comprehend.
The first time Sett had seen it, his father had pointed out
the black clumps of buffalo. The last time he himself
pointed out the faint dark spot of trees where the line
cabin stood on the distant sweep. He could not see it
now in the early morning before sunrise, but the craggy
line of White Buffalo Mountain scribed silver against
black. Finding his way was not a problem. It seemed the
trail was etched into his memory from all the nights in
the narrow cell, each step replayed from the day he had
so desperately sought to get to the cabin. He would be
able to sleep there. When he woke up, this nightmare
might be ended.

Sett sighed and closed his eyes. Traveling in the dark
tonight was slowing down an already long journey, but
he did not want to stop. The mare had finished her grain
and seemed eager to be on, so the pair began the long
climb across the first plateau. The going was easier, no
trees to darken the landmarks, and man and horse
coursed across the broad grassy swales in a tack like a
sailing ship across a glassy sea.

The mice were dancing all around her now, creating
enough scratching and scrabbling that she feared the
man would wake up and check the box against the wall.
The mules had finished eating and were outside the shel-

ter, their sighs telling her that they had settled down to
doze. The owl was silent, off on the wing hunting for
the mice, which ventured back to their nests with stolen
grain.

Ria lifted her hand cautiously. She placed her finger-
nails on the lid of the bin, and scratched the wood. The
mice froze. She scratched again, harder. There was no
sound from the man in the barn. Ria slowly pushed the
hinged lid up and tried to see into the darkness. She
scraped at the wood, mimicking the now silent mice. Her
eyes adjusted and she could make out the open space
above the feeder a few feet away. The tan mule turned
his head toward her, and she sat still except for the occasional flick of her nails on the lid. Slowly, taking deep
breaths, she cradled her bundle and rose out of the bin.
The lid gave a tiny groan and the mule pricked his ears.
She paused, scratched the lid one last time and raised
her knee high to step out of the bin.

There was a hollow click.

"Hold it right there." The voice was low in the darkness. Ria never took her eyes off the light place over the
stanchion. She flung the bundle over the wall and leaped
after it, her hands grasping at the boards. She kicked her
feet in an effort to roll over the wall, and the mules
spooked out into the corral. The top rail hit her in the
stomach, the smell of fresh dung assailed her nostrils,
and as she slithered over the rail, she felt a strong hand
grasp her ankle. She dangled there a moment, so close
to the forest that the trees seemed to beckon her with
the starlight behind them. Then she was roughly dragged
back into the dark barn.

The hands worked their way up her body, grasping
knee and hip and elbow until her arms were pinned behind her back. In the blackness she could smell the

breath of the man and feel the fingers icy against her wrists, but she could not hear him breathe. Her mind went numb.

"You didn't run very far away," Muldoon hissed. He pushed her down into the hay. "Don't move now. I want to get a look at you." Ria lay still, trying to catch her breath. She heard the man strike a match, and in a moment, the lantern cast its feeble glow.

"So you're Johnson's prized Injun girl. Glad I didn't shoot you." He peered at her with emotionless eyes. He holstered the pistol and leaned back to study her. "What are you doing here?"

Ria did not move. She stared back and willed herself not to flinch.

"I said, what are you doing here? What was that you threw over the wall?"

She said nothing.

"How long you been in here?" Muldoon clenched his jaw and squinted at the silent girl. He suddenly reached down and grasped her poncho, pulling her up from the floor. "Answer me, you little bitch. I know you speak English."

Ria stared him deep in the eyes. They were colorless, cold and glittering. She searched the hardness of them, the blank wall of soul, searching for a pocket of humanity.

The man dropped her.

He turned his back and paced across the barn. As he reached the door, Ria dashed for the partition. Her toe was on the rail, and he yanked her back again.

"You're not going anywhere."

Ria struggled to catch her breath. If she could only get out into the night, into the trees and boulders that would protect her. She glared at the quick man.

"Have you been with Foster?" He bent down to look her in the face. His mouth curled up into what tried to be a smile. " 'Cause if you have, Johnson is going to kill him." Ria took a last deep breath and set her jaw into a neutral position. Muldoon waited, waited for expression. The big doe eyes gazed off at the rafters. *The whore.* He shoved her back into the stall.

She fell against the manger, and curled there while he paced without taking his eyes off her. She made herself small, trying to blend into the flickering shadows of the lantern and the stillness of the night. Muldoon stalked left, then right. Finally he came to a stop and leaned over to glare her in the face.

"What did you throw over the wall?" He received no response. In exasperation, he pulled his bandanna from around his neck and grabbed her wrists. Binding them, he drew her arms up to the tie ring, and she lay sprawled in the hay, hanging from the manger.

"You might as well tell me. I'm going to find out." He stared at her a moment, but Ria only met him with silence. Then he climbed into the mule's shelter.

He returned with the bundle.

"Planning a trip, were you?" He shook out the blankets to reveal the sack of beans and corn, the blankets and the pots.

"Running off with Sett Foster?" Muldoon kneeled down at the end of the stall. "Where is he? Is he waiting for you?" The girl said nothing. Muldoon's face grew florid, and he grabbed her ankle and twisted her leg until she winced. "Where is he?"

Ria focused again on his face. Her mind swam from the pain, but she refused. She would not speak to this snake man. She did not have his answer anyway. She

did not know where Sett Foster was, or Coy, or Poke
Miller. Her options lay only with herself.

Muldoon released her leg. "Well, Augie will be glad
to have you back. He's missed you. But maybe I will
taste what he has been bragging about." Muldoon
moved back and examined her. She was so small her
doeskin poncho hid her form. He pulled his knife from
its sheath, and grasping the hem, slit it up the front. Ria
swallowed, and felt the cold air against her breasts.

"Hmmm," Muldoon appraised her. He leaned down
and cut the thong that held her leggings, pulling them
off in one motion. She did not flinch, did not utter a
sound. Her eyes bore into his, dark and accusing.

"A different piece of meat on the same platter," he
said.

The memory jumped to his mind: the pale flesh, the
cotton chemise, the golden hair. He unbuttoned his trousers and crawled onto her, his weight stretching her arms
in their bindings. She yielded, her body willed into obe-
dience and motionless. He thrust at her, grasped her hair
and pulled her head back, but she made no sound. She
refused to give him the satisfaction of her pain. For a
moment, he was still, then the memory called again and
he was hearing the cries of the other one, the blond girl
pleading for help. His anger at Ria's lack of response
slammed out of him, and with a groan he collapsed
against her, his weight bearing down on her shoulders
until they protested of being pulled from their sockets.

She lay still. She could smell him, the sebaceous scent
clinging to her and the weight of him becoming un-
bearable. It was not the searing burn between her legs,
or the stretching of the ligaments in her shoulders. It
was the constricting of her chest around the wildly beat-

ing heart. The pale-eyed man's head was next to hers, his ear at her lips.

"I will kill you."

He leaned back, looked deep into the fiery brown eyes.

"So you can speak." Then he groped for his pistol. He struck her on the temple, and she went slack.

ELEVEN

The colors were changing from silver to gold and the sun teased the horizon as Sett splashed down through the rushing stream and noticed the icicles bobbing on the edge of the water. The air was thin and sharp and his fatigue was replaced by a light-headed giddiness as the mare plunged up the muddy bank and out of the willows. A tiny meadow greeted them, marshy and deep green with the buds of spring. The grove of white-trunked aspen grew out of the stones of the changing creek bed. The water cascaded in a fan, offshoots of the main branch overflowing with the snowmelt. As if a natural feature, the line cabin sat with its back to the shoulder of the mountain, its construction part log, part earth and part stone. Sett rode across the marsh and dismounted at the door. It was stuck, unused and jammed as the logs settled.

He went around the corner, to the gated entry into the stall, and with a good shove was able to swing the sagging poles open. The dim interior smelled unused, except for maybe a packrat in the corner. The mare snorted and had to be coaxed in, but she settled as Sett removed her saddle and poured grain into the manger. Then he sought a toehold and climbed over the manger into the dark cabin.

To conserve heat and time this high in the mountains, the building was both cabin and barn. At one side of the tiny room was a potbelly shepherd's stove. At the other the horses hung their heads over a pallet against the wall. Sett tried the stuck door from the inside and this time it dragged open on its leather hinges. The shutters over the small window were nailed in place, slats of aspen saplings that leaked strips of light onto the packed earth floor. Sett had no idea how old the cabin was, but he remembered being fascinated by the strange dwelling when he first saw it. When he accompanied Talking Crow and his people to the crest of the pass, the old man had pointed out the cabin and chuckled as he told the tale of its builder, a French trapper. "Frenchman not smart enough to go down into the valleys for winter!"

It was just one of the many exciting places that young Sett had seen on that journey: the cairns that marked the ancient trail, the awe-inspiring view from the summit, Talking Crow gesturing into the distance as he explained the routes of the canyons below and the landmarks to follow when and if Sett ever wanted to visit the Blackfeet. The skinny boy had watched from the windy pass as his friends, a small band of warriors and women, made their way down into the forest on the other side, the old man on the black pony taking up a position at the rear. Sett had waved as the figures receded into the trees, and if Talking Crow had noticed, he did not wave back. It was then, when all the world lay unknown between him and the horizon, that Sett vowed to himself that he would go over that pass. But that day, the prom-

ise to return to his family drew him back, and only the
view from the top of the mountain remained to trick him
into twisting his life.

Now Sett wondered if he had been the last to use the
line cabin, but even after his flight and banishment, his
father and brother must have come up to check the summer pastures. And the posse had stopped here. There
was no sign that it had been used recently, though, and
this eased Sett a bit. Augie Johnson must not know it
was here.

Sett knocked the mouse nest out of the stovepipe and
started a fire. The sun was shining in the door and the
dust that he disturbed as he shook off the pallet and
unpacked his saddlebags glittered like stardust. The chill
was off the air inside now, and Sett rolled the saddle
blankets out as a mattress, spread his bedroll on top and
crawled gratefully into his bed. The mare hung her head
over him, lower lip sagging as she dozed, and he slipped
into a deep and welcome sleep.

Muldoon stepped out casually into the bright morning
sunlight. He pulled the barn door closed behind him. He
had timed it just right. There was Augie coming out of
the cabin, shaking his head.

"Good morning," Muldoon said congenially. "I fed
your stock for you."

Augie stopped and waited. "Thanks, Cap'n. Connie's
fixing breakfast." He made a face. "Then I guess I better hitch up the wagon. She's determined to go to Miller's and wait for the next freight wagon into Verdy."

"We got plenty to do. We need to find Foster, keep
an eye on him until he leads us to the gold."

"And my girl."

Muldoon nodded. Old single-minded Johnson. No

point in arguing, but it had occurred to him as he lowered the bound and gagged girl back into the grain bin
that this was getting too messy.

If the women made it to Verdy, there would likely be
a vigilante posse heading out to find Sett Foster. More
people to work around and less time to attend to the
important matters. He had to find that gold and be on
his way, preferably without Johnson.

"After you drive the ladies into the post, we'll start
tracking Foster from the camp," he said and followed
Augie into the cabin.

The little blue dog stretched her neck to see over the tall
grass in the meadow. She sat on her haunches and raised
her pointy muzzle to gather the breezes.

There was no doubt.

She looked up the slope, sampled the wind again and
held her sensitive nose to the trail.

Yes, the girl was back there, at the cabin.

And the man with the horse was off there, yonder.

Coy scratched at a tick, enjoying the itch. Then she
stood and trotted back down the trail.

Poke left at dawn, and by the time he reached the beaver
pond camp, the sun had crawled into the canyon but
there was still ice on the edges of the stream. He dismounted away from the cold fire pit and examined the
cacophony of footprints in the mud.

Sett left by choice, that was evident. All his gear was
gone and his boot prints lay on top of the two other pair.
His big mare's tracks were with his. Poke sighed in relief. He carefully kept his horse on the mat of grass in
the little meadow. He walked the perimeter of the camp.

There, at the edge of the mud, was one small moccasin print. Ria had been here before him.

Poke stepped carefully around the log bench, over the trench that drained the tent flat.

Sett was gone. Maybe gone for good. He had packed up and disappeared into the mountains and the last time he had done that Poke had been questioned hard by Moses Foster, and later by a man wearing a badge and backed up by a dozen hard riders.

He told them nothing.

Not that he didn't remember the white-haired man, or the argument between the outlaws. No, just that Ben, in his ten-year-old stubbornness, declared he didn't know nothing, and Ben right then was the only brother-link left.

Poke wondered sometimes, how his mother and father could only be granted one child, when they had the love for dozens. The Foster brood were the siblings he never had; the honorary cousins, playmates and cohorts. Then Sett left.

For days Poke had looked for a sign. Questioned as he was by the adults, he searched secretly for a clue. Not to where. He knew where, or at least, with whom. But to why. Maybe he had never stopped looking until that strangely familiar form had stepped through the door of the post the other day.

This time was different, though. This time he knew where Sett was heading, even if he didn't know if he'd be back. Would Sett leave, really leave, again without even saying good-bye? Poke furrowed his brow as he scanned the empty campsite. There was not much point in trying to track Sett Foster. He would only leave a trail if he wanted to be followed. Maybe Samantha was right.

Maybe Sett was better off on his own. Maybe Sett knew it and that was why he left.

But what about the girl? Poke went back around the bare earth to the moccasin prints. She was not hard to track. She had checked the camp last night and then returned to where she had left Roanie. Poke gathered up his horses and followed the trail up the canyon.

The door to the cabin was open and Johnson and the gunslinger were standing in the yard. They were conversing in voices too low for Poke to hear. Then Johnson turned toward the corral and the thin man went into the barn and returned with the harness. As they harnessed up a mule, the Johnson women came out, carrying bundles and dressed in bonnets and traveling dresses. Poke watched until the mule was hooked up and the women were ready in the seat of the buckboard. Then Augie mounted the other mule and waved to the man standing at the door of the cabin. He called, "Be back as soon as I get 'em through the trees, Cap'n." The faint voice carried up to Poke, and the wagon and outrider started down the trail.

Poke went back to Ria's trail, now skirting the cabin clearing and heading up into the brush. He watched for the hoofprints, but his mind was occupied with the departure of Johnson and his wife and daughter. Something must be up. He wondered what it meant, and was startled when his saddle horse raised her head and nickered. There was an answer from the trees, and Poke reined up. He listened carefully, and the hidden horse whinnied again. Riding forward into the brush, he saw Roanie, tied securely and very glad to see her barn mates.

•　•　•

Footsteps coming across the barn floor and the jingling of a harness being lifted down from its peg sifted into her conscious, pulling her, dreamlike, back to the dark and dusty grain bin. Ria tried to open her mouth, lick her dry lips, but the gag reminded her of the pale-eyed man and she froze. The footsteps receded and the barn door slammed closed. She flexed her arms, a burn of pain as the circulation returned to her hands below the tight bindings. She could hardly breathe, and as she struggled to inhale, she felt the cracking of the clotted blood and the warmth of fresh as it ran from her nose. Her left eye would not open; it throbbed when she tried. She shifted her legs in the cramped space, the ache in her hips and the twinge in her thighs bringing all of reality back for a brief moment before she slipped back into unconsciousness.

Poke stepped down and walked over to his horse. The stocky gelding pulled at the bridle reins, knotted around a limb. It was not the way you would leave a horse except for a few minutes, but there were several piles of manure and the leaves were disturbed from his pawing. Poke looked around the brushy hiding spot. The girl had planned on being gone a short time, but where was she? Poke stroked Roanie's face absentmindedly, his thoughts sorting things out. Then he untied the horse and led all three back down the canyon to the stream. After Roanie had a long drink, Poke tied him and the packhorse in another grove. It was time to pay a neighborly visit to the Johnson cabin.

Muldoon looked up startled from the springbox. All he wanted was to draw some water and shave, but there was the aggravating storekeep riding into the yard. *What next?* he thought as Poke reined up.

"Howdy." Poke nodded.

"Hello." Muldoon's eyes flicked out to the edge of the clearing, to the barn, to the cabin door where his gunbelt hung on the back of the chair. Poke enjoyed the man's discomfiture, caught here in his undershirt and without his guns. Poke smiled and crossed his hands casually over the saddle horn.

"Nice day."

"Yes." Muldoon returned to lifting the bucket out of the spring.

"Johnson here?" Poke followed on his horse as Muldoon carried the water back to the cabin. There was a steaming pan on the washstand outside the door, and Muldoon scooped the cold water into it and tested it with his little finger.

"No, you just missed him."

"The ladies not here either?"

Muldoon cast an irritated glance at him. "No, they're probably talking the ears off your women about now. Johnson took them to your place."

"We like customers!" Poke declared, a cheery expression on his face.

"No. Johnson wanted them to be someplace safe. They're going to Verdy with the next freighter." Muldoon started to lather the shaving soap with a brush, whisking it around in the pewter cup until Poke could smell the scent of it on the clear morning air.

"Well, they are in luck. A freighter's due through tomorrow, but I don't know if I'd send my family to Verdy to be safe." Poke chuckled. "It's safer out here with the bear and snakes."

"And outlaws," Muldoon said. All this cheerful banality did not add up. He wished his gun was not hanging on the chair.

"Nah, if there was an outlaw around here, I'd know! I know everybody in this country." Poke saw Muldoon glance again at his gunbelt hanging just out of reach on the chair. If the Johnson women were at the post, he'd better get on back and make sure things were OK. Still, he wished there were some sign of Ria. The cabin seemed empty, and the garden plot sat neglected, the few tiny shoots of the new plants withering from lack of water.

Muldoon daubed the lather on his face, and selected his razor from the kit. "There you are wrong. The outlaw is here. He came into the yard and threatened the Johnson women."

Poke watched the man calmly draw the razor over his face, the careful upstrokes under the chin and delicate carving around the mustache.

"Actually, I'm looking for a horse. Roan gelding, freshly shod. Seen him?"

"Wandered off?" Muldoon dabbed at his face with a sacking cloth, and checked his job in the mirror.

"Nope. He was stolen."

"Really?" Now Muldoon stepped back toward the door and pulled on his shirt. Poke had the sudden urge to get out of the yard, like his grudging welcome was about to give out.

"How do you know?"

"I was there," Poke said flatly.

"Who did it?" Muldoon slid the gunbelt off the chair and around his hips and buckled it. He took his coat down from the peg by the door and tapped the dust off of his round hat.

"Little half-breed girl."

Muldoon stopped in his tracks. "A girl."

"Yep. Johnson's girl." Poke stared at him.

"She was alone?"

"Yes. Very alone."

"Haven't seen her." Muldoon returned to collecting his gear. "Johnson's told me all about her though. Seems she ran off with the outlaw. Bet that's where you'll find your horse, if you care to take on the Boy Stage Robber."

"There's no reason to take on Sett Foster." Poke gathered up his reins as Muldoon closed the cabin door and started across to the corral to catch up his horse. "He's no more outlaw than you or me."

"That so?" Muldoon turned his back on Poke to swing the gate.

"Besides, the girl isn't with him."

"I'll keep my eyes open."

Poke turned his horse and started to walk out of the yard.

Muldoon was wiping off his studhorse's back and tossing on the saddle. He said over his shoulder, "This Foster, he's a friend of yours?"

"Everyone around here knows Sett Foster," Poke answered.

"Tell him I have the information he seeks. We got to meet alone, without Johnson."

Poke slowed his horse. The sun was halfway to noon, and the shadow of the barn huddled deep and dark on the north side. There, panting in the tall grass, was the blue bitch, her pointy coyote nose pressed to a gap in the log wall.

"I'll tell him."

• • •

Samantha Miller could not help glancing across the valley every time she passed the window as she went about her chores. Poke was gone at dawn, packing extra supplies on the sale horse and riding her saddle horse. She and Mother Abby had helped him pack: travel food for several days, extra blankets, bandages, a short shovel and tarp. He had tried to sneak the ammunition into his pocket, hoping they did not see as he scooped the boxes of cartridges off the shelf in the soddy store. She had watched him out of sight as the sun rose over the Cottonwoods, and she was still watching hours later.

The children were working at their lessons, reading out of *Gray's Primer,* and Mother Abby was listening to Gail sail through chapter nine as she worked on darning an old sock by feel. Samantha paused at the cabin door.

"I'm going to see if there are any eggs," she announced and the children and her mother-in-law stared up at her. Gathering the eggs was Gail's chore, done every morning after milking the cow.

Samantha needed to get out of the house. She took a deep breath and crossed the yard. Her stomach was churning. It felt like when Jeanette was kicking so violently in there. She held a hand to her belly and started across the yard to the chicken coop. Perspiration broke out on her face and she stopped at the stock trough to lean against its solid side. She wet her hand and smoothed the cool across her brow. The road in the distance quivered in the bright light of the noonday sun and she squinted at the dark moving object.

Customers. Just what she did not need right now.

Samantha started for the soddy store. With Poke away, she would have to be the shopkeeper, and this looked like a farm wagon and not mounted Indians or cowboys. She unlatched the door and left it wide to indicate that the Post was open for business, then she leaned against the counter and inhaled the cool air. The little room smelled of tobacco and earth, with the stinging scent of vinegar from the pickle barrel in the corner. Her stomach settled and she decided that it must be her nerves. The wagon seemed to be taking a long time to come into the yard, and after straightening the counter and wiping the pervading dust from the jars of preserves, she went to the door.

The wagon was stopped across the river, above the mushy bank to the ford. It looked odd because there was only one mule hitched up, and it was balking at the muddy descent into the water. Samantha stepped out into the sunlight and the driver of the wagon stood up and waved a handkerchief.

"Yoo-hoo! Yoo-hoo!" The woman's voice carried clearly over the running water. "Is it safe to cross?"

Samantha walked out toward the river. The crazy woman was still standing in the wagon and the mule was pawing.

"Sit down!" Samantha called to her.

"I said is it safe to cross?"

Samantha's soft voice must not have carried. Abby and the girls came out onto the porch. Samantha motioned broadly with her arm. "Sit down!" She yelled again. Then she waved the two women toward the ford. The driver sat quickly as the mule began to turn, then she heaved on the rein. As the mule swung back to the crossing, the passenger clung to the seat and the driver slapped the rein. The mule began to wade through the knee-deep water.

Gail appeared by her side and Samantha laid her hand on her daughter's shoulder.

"They will need help with the mule. Something must be wrong."

"I can take care of it," the girl said.

As the dripping wagon pulled up in the yard, the pale-faced passenger gathered her skirts and clambered over the side.

"Oh, we made it. We made it."

Samantha inspected her. Other than her sickly complexion, she seemed hale. The older woman stiffly climbed to the ground and walked away from the wagon without a backward glance. She came up to Samantha.

"You must be Mrs. Miller. I'm Mrs. Johnson, and this is my daughter, Carolyn."

Samantha nodded to her and to the girl, who reached for her hand and clung to it. "Oh, it is so good to see another civilized face. We did not think we would make it. What a frightful journey!"

Samantha tried to withdraw her hand and looked again for signs of injury or attack. The pair seemed healthy, and were quite well dressed. Samantha frowned.

"What happened? Were you attacked?"

"Oh no, but we could have been, all alone out there with wild Indians and stage robbers!" Carolyn glanced back over her shoulder as if pursued.

Samantha eyed Mrs. Johnson, who was patting her daughter's back soothingly. Gail led the mule away, and pulled a box out of the barn to stand on while she unbuckled the harness. Neither woman made any motion to help. There was a cardboard suitcase in the wagon, and a flour sack stuffed with personal items. Samantha's stomach gave another heave and she asked, "Stage robbers, did you say?"

"Yes, there is an outlaw on the loose out there, the Boy Stage Robber, they say, all grown up now! He is armed and dangerous. We came here to beg refuge until the next freighter can take us to Verdy." Mrs. Johnson stood very straight. There was no way Millers could refuse two neighbor women in desperate need, even if Augie did describe them as being less than friendly.

"He is very dangerous!" Carolyn broke in. "We saw him. He came right into the yard. He sneaked up on us. Who knows what would have happened! Then he stole our girl and tried to shoot at Pa! Captain Muldoon says he's a killer. He looked like one, he—"

"There was shooting? When?" Samantha cut her off.

Mrs. Johnson answered, "Almost. My husband and Captain Muldoon went to talk with him about returning the girl and he held the rifle on them. Today they were going out after him and I thought we would not be safe by ourselves in the cabin. We wish to go on to Helena as soon as possible. We hear they have a lawman there." Samantha wondered if they thought that having a peace officer really meant that the burgeoning city of Helena was peaceful.

"And there was a kidnapping?" She tried to sort the pieces into Poke's story.

"Well, he stole our girl, our . . . maid." Mrs. Johnson seemed uncomfortable with this detail. She gave her daughter a warning look when the girl opened her mouth to speak. Samantha pursed her lips. Samantha felt an instant dislike of these two big blond women, especially since little Gail was hanging up the harness and turning the mule into the corral without so much as a thank-you.

"Jack Cody is due through tomorrow. He could show you the way to Verdy. Please, come up to the house."

Constance and Carolyn followed her across the yard, leaving the suitcase in the wagon.

•   •   •

"You have such a lovely home, Mrs. Miller. Your little store must be quite profitable." Constance set her coffee cup back on the table and sighed. From the sideboard by the stove, Samantha spooned the dried-apple cobbler onto the plates.

"It provides a living," she answered mildly. Constance Johnson had not moved from her chair since entering the house. The daughter was snoring away on the pallet, where she had reclined after eating the meal Samantha prepared. Samantha delivered the plate to the table.

"Of course, it was yours first!" Constance turned and shouted at Mother Abby.

"My eyes are weak, not my ears," the old woman said quietly. Constance went on full voiced.

"How nice of your son to let you stay here and care for you in your old age!" She began to spoon the dessert into her mouth. "Where is Mr. Miller?" She looked around as if he was hiding in the room and she'd just realized it. Samantha paused with her back to her guest. Gail stared at this rude stranger before remembering it was not polite to stare. Mother Abby clenched her jaw another degree tighter.

She had said very little since the Johnson women arrived. There had not been much room to talk, but with all the chattering these two did she had learned more than she would have thought to ask. Samantha was upset; Abby could hear her heels on the floorboards as she worked in the kitchen, and judge the polite distance in her voice. Samantha had not wanted Poke to leave. Abby had heard them arguing last night. This story the Johnsons had to tell was not relieving her daughter-in-law's stress.

Samantha straightened. "Poke isn't here right now, he's . . ."

"Out hunting," Abby said firmly.

Samantha looked Constance Johnson in the eyes. "Yes. He went hunting."

"Oh, men do that, don't they? August spends all his time hunting. He is never home! Sometimes he is gone for days. Of course that was not a problem when we had the girl." Constance mopped up the last of the cobbler and handed her plate to Gail, who put it in the wash pan and went outside to the washstand. Samantha lifted the kettle of hot water off the stove and followed.

Abby stood up and began tapping her way to the door. "Here, Samantha, I'll help dry."

"I think Carolyn has the right idea. I'm going to lay down and take a nap." Constance stretched.

Samantha dropped the tin plate into the pan with a clang.

"I cannot believe these people!" She whispered to Abby, "What are we going to do?"

"We are going to pray that Jack Cody gets here tomorrow," Abby whispered back.

"But what if Poke returns with Sett?"

"Samantha, we have nothing to fear from Sett Foster. I'm sure of that." Samantha did not answer. Abby heard her silence. "I'm not saying he isn't a dangerous man, just that he would never harm us."

"If Sett Foster comes here, he will draw all his problems right to our yard. Poke is out there with him this minute, putting himself out to get shot! He doesn't have to mean to harm us." Samantha fought to keep her voice under control. "Mother Abby, I don't know what to think. I know Poke wants us to side with Foster, but what these women said . . ."

.

"You can't put too much faith into what these two say, can you? They only care about their own comfort, and they have no idea what their men are up to." Abby handed a dried bowl to Gail, who was taking in the grown-up conversation with big eyes. "We have to stick together. Don't say much and listen a lot. Tomorrow they can leave with Jack Cody. It's Poke's decision where his allegiance lies."

Samantha sighed and handed over another plate.

Gail watched her mother's worried face. It was not like her mother to lie, but Gail knew some of what had been said was different from what her parents had told her. And she had a question.

"Did Mr. Foster really steal a little girl?"

Samantha knelt down to hug her daughter. "No, honey, I don't think he stole her. I think he might have helped her get away."

"Get away from what?"

Her mother looked up at her grandmother.

"She was a slave," Abby stated.

"So she had to work for them all the time?"

"There is a lot to being a slave and none of it good, child." Abby finished drying the last plate.

TWELVE

Sett had his hand on the hilt of the knife before he opened his eyes. His body reacted before his mind could struggle out the details of where he was. His sight adjusted and the realization of the line shack brought the fleeting edge of panic. He scanned the dim room, where just moments before Whitey and Jed had been arguing and the Tejano cleaning his rifle.

There was no one.

The mare was watching him with big dark eyes, and Sett sighed and relaxed down into the blankets.

It was a dream, just another dream. He wondered how long he had slept. The light angling in the open door was filtered by shade and the room was warm. He should get up and eat something, maybe scout around a bit and put the mare out to graze. Instead he folded his hands behind his head and turned his mind loose.

It had been a nightmare. The last time he had stared up at this ridge pole with its hatchet-marked sapling rafters leaking dust from the sod roof, he had been terrified. He'd sought safe refuge, the comforting familiar, trans-

portation home. Instead he huddled in the corner and
listened to Jed.

"We'd be in the clear, we'd be on our way to Alberta,
if you hadn't shot that driver." Jed spat tobacco in the
corner near the stable. "Damn it, Whitey, couldn't you
control your temper?"

"What are you complaining for? We got the money."

"All of the territory will be after us. They get robbed
all the time, but killing in cold blood . . ."

"We ain't caught yet. The boy here knows the way
over the mountains, don't you, boy?" Sett felt the ice-
blue eyes on him and the pressure that they contained.
There was a northwest wind blowing; this time of year
it meant snow. The aspen outside the line shack were
bare. He had never seen them like that this early. It was
winter in the high country and one would be a fool to
dare the pass now.

Whitey asked again, "You know the way?"

Sett nodded.

He had known the way, right up to the blanketing
snowstorm that walled off the pass and left him wandering in circles to lead the group right into the posse's
camp. Not that he had been unhappy to see it, the flickering light of fires and the glow of tents promising survival through the night, and also the survival of what
was to come. But at the moment that Whitey asked him
the question, he had just wished to find reality a bad
dream.

The mare shook her head, flopping her ears in annoyance. Sett sighed and sat up.

"OK, big mare, I'll put you out."

Sett found the hobbles in his saddlebags and climbed
into the stall. Once out in the meadow, the mare
searched out the muddiest spot on the creek bank and

lay down to roll, her satisfied groans bringing a smile to the man's face. He paused to look down the breaks, the late morning sunlight stealing the shadows. The nightmares seemed long distant now, but the truth was right behind him. Sett rested his eyes on the ridges to the south. He could not see any movement in the pass, no one following from Buffalo Canyon. At least not yet. Surely Poke had found the abandoned camp, but whether he would try to find Sett or just wait for him to come into the Post remained to be seen. Sett wondered about the girl, about the reception she would get from Mother Abby and Poke's wife, Samantha. And if she would stay put until he got back. Maybe he should have made her promise. Maybe he should have promised.

He went in and got his rifle and cleaning kit, and his pouch with the Arkansas stone, then chose a shady spot under the aspens. First he tested his skinning knife with his thumb and put it aside. He tested the little short blade that hid in the sheath on the back of his belt, and the penknife that he carried in his trouser pocket. With a view of the bay mare grazing among the purple iris and the green and gold plateaus stretching down in front of him, he lay out his rags, canteen and stone and began to sharpen his knives.

Ria opened her right eye in surprise. The blackness of the grain bin flickered a moment, bright spots of color twirling against the lid. She held her breath, ears straining for the sound that had brought her back to consciousness. Once again she stretched each finger and toe, hoping to find all working. There was no clue to how long she had been in the bin, no true light to fall across her world.

There, again, was a creak. The barn door was shifting

on its hinge. Ria felt a hint of breeze through the cracks between the boards. She closed her eye and concentrated on her breathing. Best to make it light and even. She wondered where her knife was, still in the clothing or taken by the gun-man? She balled her hands into a double fist, braced what felt like her good leg against the corner of the box and waited. Footfalls crossed the packed dust floor, and a panting breath came just outside. The little sniff and chortle, then a *hmmmmm* of a whine. Ria tried to say "Coy?" just as the lid opened.

In the sudden burst of light a man's head and shoulders were framed in the opening. Ria swung her bound fists up and cuffed him alongside the ear.

"Damn you, little heathen!" Poke flinched from the blow and grabbed her hands. He stared down into the grain bin. She lay there staring back, bruises deeper than the shadows, a dark stain of blood across her mouth and jaw.

"Oh my god," Poke whispered. "Are you all right?" He leaned back down and fumbled with the gag. Now Ria shrank back from him. When her mouth was free, she licked her lips and tried to speak, but no words would come. She heard the whine again, and her eye followed the sound.

"I wouldn't have found you except for the dog." Poke reached down to help her out of the bin. "We got to get you out of here."

Poke scooped her up and started for the door. It was like carrying his daughter, so light was she in his arms. Coy following anxiously behind.

"No. No." Ria struggled against him. Poke set her down on her feet, the loose clothing falling to the barn floor. The girl stooped to gather up the loose shirt and wrap it around her, using her belt with the pouch and knife sheath to cinch it shut. Then she sat in the dirt floor to tie on the moccasins. Coy came over to nose into her hand. Ria stopped her hurried dressing and stroked the stand-up ears.

"We need to be going." Poke glanced at the door. Ria tried to rise, but failed, and Poke lent a firm grasp to her arm.

"Can you ride?"

"Yes."

In the daylight she looked even worse than she had inside. Poke tried not to stare at her face, not to let her see the damage reflected in his eyes. He hoisted her onto Roanie's saddle and took the reins as he mounted his horse.

"I will ride," the girl said hoarsely. She looked at the reins in his hand with her good eye. Poke judged her with the sun slanting over her shoulder. She was still small, still bruised and bloody, with the flow renewing itself from her nose. Her bare legs hung down with just the toes in the stirrups, the bundle of her clothing held securely in front of her. She held out her hand, the slim fingers scabbed from an older injury. *She will do what-ever she wants to, I guess,* Poke thought to himself. He flipped the reins over the gelding's neck and handed them to her.

"Where is the gun-man?" she whispered. She scanned the yard.

"Left a while ago with Augie. Looking for Sett." Poke watched her tighten her jaw as she moved her head.

"Where is Sett?"

Poke swallowed. "I'm not sure. I think I know where he went."

Poke started for the trees, and the girl followed. Once

in the cover, he angled down the canyon, staying well
above the wagon road. He wanted to get back home as
soon as possible, but what if Muldoon or Augie had
circled back? At the junction of the cemetery trail, he
paused. The path that had been unused for so long now
looked like a highway. The deep mulch beneath the
pines was plowed and scarred by the hurried passing of
many hooves over the last few days. All going up. The
girl gazed up the trail. She looked back at Poke.

"You need to get to the post. Sam can help you."
Poke did not like the way she stared at him. The stillness
of her face left her thoughts rather clear. "Damn it, girl,
you are in no shape to go running off after Sett. He
doesn't need to worry about you right now."

"I am going," Ria stated quietly.

"Take it from me, you are not going to make it over
the mountains alone in that condition. Besides, that's my
horse." Poke gritted his teeth. "We don't have time for
this. We got to get you to the post so I can go help
Sett."

Ria nodded as if that were the answer she was waiting
for, and she turned Roanie to follow the tracks up the
cemetery trail.

Foster's trail was slow to follow, and Augie's mind
drifted to searching for a sign of the gold's hiding place.
Muldoon was a better marksman than scout. Here he
went slowly, knowing a mounted man had to leave some
trail, but surprised at Foster's deceptions. His search
veered up and down the hillside.

"There's on old Injun trail over the pass goes through
here," Augie commented. "I think he's headed that
way."

"Familiar with it?"

"I only been up to the head of the canyon. They say the Injuns used to run buffalo up there." Augie scratched his chin. "There's old blazes on the trees in places."

Muldoon reined up. "Johnson, was that an idea that just floated out of your head?"

Johnson opened his mouth and stared at the cap'n. "What?"

"This would go a lot faster if we could just follow a trail. Where are the blazes?"

Johnson pointed. "Down along the creek. I followed 'em thinking they'd lead to the gold. You know. But I stopped at the top of the canyon. Ran out of supplies."

Muldoon considered the last place he had found a track, in the mud on one of the numerous creek crossings. "And he's following it so far?"

"Seems so."

Muldoon headed down toward the creek bank. He could hardly see the scar on the bark of the pine when Augie pointed it out. The cut was so old it had healed over, the light pebbly texture being the only visible difference.

"How'd you even see that?" He squinted in surprise at dumb August Johnson.

"I was looking for a marker to the gold."

Muldoon made a quick search of the ground. In the gravel by the water was a scuff. A large animal had come through there this morning. A large shod animal.

"It may be just that," Muldoon said as they continued up Buffalo Canyon.

Poke caught up with Ria at the cemetery clearing. She had stopped Roanie and was leaning over in the saddle as if to catch her breath.

"See, I told you you're in no condition to head off here."

She sat up, but kept her face turned away. He could barely hear her choked voice.

"Which one is the sister?" She inclined her head carefully toward the silent gray headboards.

"This one."

She rode around to face the grave. "That is her name, the markings on the board?"

"Yes. Elizabeth." Poke rode over beside her. The blackened eye was nearest him, so swollen that it barely opened. "Come to the post with me. I promise you'll be safe." She did not move. "It is the best way to help Sett."

Now she faced him, her good eye as deep and silent as a dark and muddy river.

"I am going."

Poke's mild face erupted with anger. "You are going? Just where are you going? You think you can ride off with my horse, go bumbling into the middle of a fray, head over the mountain? Exactly where is it you are going?"

Ria did not flinch. Her black eye widened a bit, and she gazed on this mad white man as if he could not hear, or was too dumb to understand. Then she pointed north to the pass through Buffalo Canyon.

THIRTEEN

Following the blazes was much easier going. Augie sighted the marked trees, and Muldoon scanned the ground for tracks. The old trail wound up the canyon, twisting back and forth through the dwindling waters of the creek as it bounced against the sheer walls. Large cottonwoods crowded the bottom, and pines swayed on up the slope. Augie's mule forged along unguided, following the easiest path. Muldoon spotted the occasional hoofprint and wondered about Augie's theory about the blazes leading to the gold.

It looked like they would find Sett Foster, for sure. His trail now seemed ridiculously simple. Muldoon glared at Johnson's lumpy back as the mule pulled up the grade. It would not be good for Johnson to meet up with Foster first. He stroked his lip thoughtfully.

Johnson had taken the edited version of Poke Miller's visit as planned—outraged that Foster had not only taken his girl, but was a horse thief as well. Meeting up with him on the road, and suggesting they take off immediately on Foster's trail, had worked without a hitch, but now this was taking way longer than he had expected. And somehow he had to get rid of Johnson and talk to Foster alone.

That thorny bush occupied Muldoon until the canyon opened up onto the first of the plateaus, the trees fading out into the grassland, and the easy marked trail disappearing into the breaks.

Augie pulled the mule to a stop.

"Cap'n?" He indicated the great open space with a tilt of his head.

"This is as far as you came before?"

"A little farther. There's cairns. I followed 'em about a mile or so. That way." The creek branched off, main stream trickling from the north and its tributary joining from slightly west.

"We might as well ride up that way. But keep your eyes open." Muldoon urged his horse.

The first cairn was a large one, built on the low bluff of the creek forks. The rocks were tumbled in a pile, each branch of the creek pointed to with a smaller line of stones radiating out from the base.

"Which way?" Muldoon asked.

"That looks like the main trail."

Muldoon searched the distant reaches of his view. This was an easy place to lose a man, he thought, especially one that wanted to be lost. He cursed silently to himself. "Might as well follow that for a ways."

The afternoon thunderheads were gathering up on the mountaintop, blowing in great dark shapes across the sky. The sun suddenly died, blotches of shadow staining the golden plains below. Sett finished cleaning his rifle and leaned back on the aspen trunk. The moving clouds made it difficult to see the lower plateaus. A herd of antelope grazed undisturbed in the distance, and he took his comfort that there were no pursuers yet.

Sett closed his eyes. Weariness settled on him again, but he did not want to sleep. He did not want to have to out-ride the ghosts.

He made himself get up. The sun was disappearing in the clouds, and if he was going to ride back to the post tomorrow, it wouldn't hurt to shave before it got dark. The stove was still warm, and the fire burst into life with the addition of a few twigs. Sett unrolled the mirror and soap from his kit. Outside, he found the pole bench between three trees, and laid out his razor, and the new block of paper-wrapped soap that Samantha had made to sell in the post. He pulled off his shirt and laid it carefully aside. The mirror hung on a limb stub, swaying gently with the tree in the gusty wind. Sett examined his face in the small square.

He felt rough: at least a week's growth of beard and long hair straggling down his neck, and dark hazel eyes that held no answer even when he stared into their depths. It was still like looking at a stranger.

He had not seen his own reflection the entire time he was in prison, until the last day, when the warden had walked with him to the barbershop in town and paid for a bath and a shave. The barber had lathered him up and shaved quickly, then done an equally fast job on his hair, finishing with a handheld mirror that revealed a man Sett didn't know. The warden had then brought him to the general store, bought him a new set of clothes, shook his hand and said, "Stay out of trouble, Foster. And get out of this town."

Sett lathered the soap into his palms, but his gaze left his own face and focused on the background. The deep green of the saltgrass in the meadow undulated in the gusting wind. The distant edge of the forest on the far slope was in a spot of sunshine, although the sky behind it was dark with thunderheads. Sett squinted at the line of trees. Had something moved?

Seconds ticked by, measured only in the pounding of the blood in his ears as he listened to the quakies chatter, and the thin clink of the mirror as it rocked on its hook. There, there it was. A small coyote. Probably out hunting before the storm. Sett turned back to the mirror, raised his hands to his stubbled jaw again and the mare let out a whispered nicker behind him in the meadow that brought him quickly around.

She was staring intently across the meadow, her large ears cocked forward and her nostrils fluttering at the scent. Sett followed her gaze, and there, shaking herself of the chill waters of the stream, was the breed girl's little dog.

Sett scanned the perimeter again as Coy trotted up to the horse and raised her nose in greeting. Then she turned and padded over to him, and sat down nearby as if she belonged.

"What are you doing here?" he asked the dog. She lolled her tongue and panted from her journey. Sett scowled at her. She should be with Ria. Sett rinsed the soap from his hands and wiped them on his jeans. Shaving forgotten, he gathered his belt and went out to have a look around.

From the wall of boulders behind the line cabin, the view of the slopes of White Buffalo Mountain was unobstructed. Sett's eyes backtracked down the creek, pausing for a moment on the lip of the canyon where the trail to the homestead wound. No movement, no movement at all. A hawk was circling, spiraling up on the draft from the canyon, still below where Sett stood in

the screen of leaves. But for the sudden appearance of
the dog, Sett could pretend that he was alone out here.
He wanted to be alone here, not seeing a ghost behind
every sway of the branches.

Coy sat beside him. He hadn't noticed her following
him up the rocks, but now he squatted down beside her
and rubbed her ears. She was recovering, not panting
like she had, and was watching the view as if as inter-
ested as he. Only she was watching in the wrong direction.

It took a moment for Sett to catch on, but there across
the meadow, coming downhill and closer than he liked,
were two riders. Sett clenched his jaw. He did not expect
anyone from that direction; all afternoon he had been
watching the backtrail to the south. He sat motionless.
One of the riders was hunched over, riding curled in the
saddle. The leader was cautiously picking the way
around the scattered boulders in the grass and across the
steep fingers of the stream. Coy gave a little whine. Sett
jumped up and started the scramble through the brush
down to the cabin.

Poke looked up from the rocks ahead of him at the noise,
and was startled to see the line cabin huddled in the
shadows of the mountain. Even knowing it was there,
he could have ridden past it, and that would have been
bad. The girl was barely conscious. He had been guiding
Roanie as carefully as he could, hoping that she could
stay aboard just a while longer, when the crashing of
brush and the pricked ears of the horses pointed out the
destination. There was Sett's big horse, hobbled in front
of the door, and Sett himself stepping out of the trees.
Poke waved his hand, sighing.

Sett met them at the last creek bank. He reached up

to slide the girl from her saddle as Roanie stopped in the yard. Poke was down from his horse and kneeling beside him as he set the girl in the grass.

"Who did this?" Sett's voice was sharp but his hands gentle as he tipped Ria's head to examine her injuries.

"I'd say Muldoon, but she hasn't said anything." Poke shook his head. "She refused to go to the post, Sett. She ran away from me right after we left you, and I didn't find her until this morning, tied up in the grain bin of the barn."

Sett glanced at his old friend. The girl murmured and rolled her head, then settled back into her deep breathing. Sett slipped his arm under her neck, and easily lifted her, carrying her down to the line cabin and the cot on the back wall.

The sky carried through on its threat in fits and gusts, first the wind rattling the leaves, then the piercing pound of hail, then a brief golden beam as the sun slipped between clouds. Muldoon and Johnson huddled under their shelter tarp against a bank, a tiny fire fighting for life in the wind. The bank behind them was already wet, and the blankets took on that stifling odor of wet wool. Muldoon peered up at the changing sky and hoped this would blow over quickly. He hated to sleep cold and wet. Johnson was sitting like a log, the only movement his jaws working away on a strip of dried jerky.

"This is not good," Muldoon said.

Johnson grunted and shrugged. "Montana weather." He pulled his neck deeper inside his coat and tore another mouthful off the meat.

"It'll wash out his tracks."

"Ain't seen any tracks for a while now."

"Where could he be?"

Augie did not answer. He leaned out and put another stick on the fire.

"I just hope he is as cold and miserable as we are," Muldoon muttered.

"Aw, this ain't bad, Cap'n. Could be snowing." Augie uncorked the canteen and took a sip, then offered it to his dismal tentmate. "We got some food, and water and the tarps. We'll make out OK. Then tomorrow we can find Foster and the girl."

"Johnson, all I want is that gold and to spend next winter in Mexico." Muldoon wiped off the mouth of the canteen before drinking.

"Well, that's good 'cause I wasn't planning on sharing the girl."

Muldoon stared straight ahead. He wondered what old Johnson would do when he found the girl wasn't with Foster. Of course, it shouldn't be a problem. At the moment though, Muldoon had little confidence that his plan would unfold as he wished. It seemed nature and circumstance were all against him.

The latest hail shower had ceased and the ground sparkled with tiny ice balls. Muldoon crawled out of the tent and stood up.

"I'll be right back. I'm going to look around while it's still light."

"I'll make some coffee." Augie started searching through his saddlebags.

Muldoon walked past the horse and mule tied in the thickets, and climbed up the muddy clay bank to the plain. The arched ridge of White Buffalo Mountain was wreathed for the moment in cobalt blue sky, the thunderheads sailing in clusters on their way east. He squinted at the skyline, ten miles distant. There were patches of green, groves of aspen, scattered among the

gray blanket of sage and dark walls of rimrocks. There
were a few antelope returning to graze on the slope
above him, and well off a coyote was beginning to call
his brothers. A huge open world, creatures and plants
living as they had for thousands of years, with no sign
of human habitation. An enormous area to be looking
for one man.

The line of the creek was easy to follow, marked with
the tall trees, and so was its twin fork that ran off west-
erly from the convergence by the cairns. The fork wound
up steeply to its headwaters just under the ridge of the
mountain. The large grove of trees crowded the rock
outcropping. No sign of habitation.

Muldoon sighed, and turned to go back to the crude
camp in the draw, then he stopped.

Squinting again up at the ridge, with the sun playing
its last light on the mountainside, he saw a flash, a twinkling signal as a mirror hung above a three-cornered
bench betrayed the whereabouts of Sett Foster.

The tiny line shack was crowded with three people and
the dog. Sett and Poke sat on the floor, cradling their
plates in their laps, in front of the potbelly stove. Ria
slept on the cot, with Coy on guard underneath. The rain
pounded on the pole-and-dirt roof, dripping through the
skimpy places, then a whistling of wind wound under
the eaves. For a long time Sett had been silent. He
forked the boiled dried elk into his mouth without tasting
it, and mopped up the juice with a chunk of travel bread.
Poke watched his friend devour the meal.

He'd come into the cabin to find Sett gently wiping
the blood off the breed girl's face. She seemed asleep,
or unconscious. Poke had not ventured close enough to

determine which. After the ride up the canyon, she had finally allowed her body its injuries.

Poke had unpacked the extra horse and hauled the supplies into the cabin. Sett had not moved from his perch on the side of the pallet.

"What did she say?"

Poke was surprised. "What?"

"What did she say? When you found her?" Sett got up from his vigil by the cot.

"Um, not much. She asked where the man with the gun was." Poke searched his memory for her words. "She said 'I'm going' and she started off after you."

"And you followed?"

"I didn't think she'd make it alone." Poke began unpacking the panniers, looking for the medicines that Mother Abby had packed, and the provisions for dinner.

"She wouldn't have had to make it if you'd brought her to the post like I'd asked."

Poke turned to stare at Sett. The hazel eyes were dark under his brow, the jaw clenched. Sett's large frame dominated the tiny room. Suddenly the idea of him in a prison cell seemed entirely plausible, as if in limited space he grew to menacing proportions. Poke carefully pulled the bandage kit from the pack bag and laid it on the floor.

"I did my best, Sett. You'll have to ask her why she didn't want to go."

"It wasn't left up to her; it was up to you."

"I doubt that." Poke turned away to look in the pannier again. He could feel Sett Foster's eyes on the back of his neck, feel the thoughts, the hatred of this brother as he searched for some way to explain all of the hurt away.

"Poke, I don't want any of you involved. As soon as

she can travel, you take her back to the post.''

Poke was silent.

"I mean it, Poke. Get her out of here. That's an innocent girl with her face all messed up, and worse. I thought I could trust you. I thought you'd take care of her.'' Sett shifted, his face contorting from hatred to pain. Poke watched the emotions streak across the grown face of the boy. He felt himself dragged along. There was more pain than anger, more regret than revenge.

Poke Miller shivered as each hair on the back of his neck twitched. *A ghost ran up my spine,* he thought. *Or the girl's awake and staring at me.*

"She wanted to know which grave was Elizabeth's,'' he blurted out suddenly. Sett leaned forward.

"Why?''

"I don't know. She just stared at the headboard, wanted to know what the words said.''

"She knows something.'' Sett glanced over at the quiet form on the cot.

"She knows who hit her,'' Poke said.

"It's more than that.''

They sat and ate in silence, Poke gauging Sett's thoughts by the changing colors of his eyes in the flickering light of the lamp. It was uncomfortable, sitting with a brother he didn't know. And at home the Johnson women were at his house—and who knew where Muldoon and Johnson were. Poke couldn't hope they were at the post; but there was only one other place they could be, and that was right outside on the trail. How far away were they? Poke tasted the last of the bitter coffee. The grit lay on his tongue, daring him to spit.

He swallowed.

"Sett, I got to go home first thing in the morning.''

Sett did not move. "That's what I said.''

"No, I got to go without the girl. Fast."

Sett Foster turned to face his boyhood friend. "Is there something you're not telling me?"

Poke paled a little. "Augie Johnson's wife and girl are at the post."

"And?"

"Either Johnson and Muldoon are on your trail this moment, or one or both of them are at the post. Sett, that girl can't travel as fast as I'm gonna be traveling."

"We'll tie her to the horse."

"Damn it, Sett! I don't know how we ended up as this girl's watch keepers, but you showed up with her first. My wife is at home with my children and a bunch of strangers. I have got to go."

"You can't leave her here with me." Sett's voice was strangled. "I can't help her."

"I can't choose her, or you, over my family." Poke leaned back and shut his eyes. He did not want to see the look on Sett's face, did not want to see pain that was becoming as familiar as the boyish grin used to be. The silence beckoned, the wood stove popped and wind whispered around the spaces in the sod eaves. The fine big mare in the stall snorted into her feed, and somewhere up the rocky cleft Poke's horses in the trees heard it and nickered.

From the cot in the corner, the blanket rustled, and when Poke and Sett turned, startled, toward it, the girl was sitting up, her one doe eye shining at them in the lamplight.

"I am staying."

FOURTEEN

The air hung heavy in the tiny room. The outlaw Sett Foster stared right into her eyes. The first flash of anger dissolved from his face and was replaced with the same composure she had seen the first time he rode into the cabin yard.

Poke Miller cast a sly glance at his friend.

She tried to remain focused on Sett, to wait as long as he waited. The shepherd's stove crackled in the corner, the room heating up as she sat. It was so hot. She wanted to open her left eye, but when she did the figures swam in the heat and her head became suddenly very heavy. Ria lifted her hand to her temple.

Sett Foster crossed the room in one catlike step and caught her hand before she could touch the damage to her face.

"Don't."

Ria swayed in front of him, fighting off the dizziness. He sat beside her on the cot and she leaned into him. His shoulder was sure against her cheek, and for a moment the scent of horses and damp cotton invaded all of her senses. Then she remembered why she was here.

She pulled back from Sett and composed the good side of her face into a serious mask. She did not want to ask, and especially not to beg. But she also did not want to be tied to the horse. If Sett Foster really wanted her gone, she assumed he could do it. Best for him if he chose not to. She said, "My grandfather is over the mountains."

"You can go to your grandfather from the post. Poke will arrange it with a freighter."

"No." Ria's vision cleared, and she caught Poke Miller's look from over Sett's shoulder. She thought, *He is an ally this time.* "Ma'am is at your post."

Poke nearly smiled at the girl. He nodded. She could not go there. They'd be sending her back to slavery.

Ria's head throbbed when she looked back to Sett. No crack in the controlled demeanor, he helped her balance against the bruise and the fever, and his quiet hands did not give away the emotion that she herself had heard.

Her fever broke in the night; and the sweat lodge of the cabin became as chill as the midnight air. Once out of the struggle for lucidity, Ria opened her eyes to utter darkness and listened to the breathings of the room; Coy's short snorts under her bed and a gentle whistling from over by the stove, and the silence of the one who was also awake, next to her cot. She began to shiver, and curled her body into a ball under the blanket.

Two days? Or three? She sorted the recent past into day and night, marking time by the events and filling in the hours she did not remember. She did not know where Muldoon was, and it irked her. She reached up in the darkness and used her fingertips to explore the mashed skin around her eye. The bone of her nose was deviated, a sharp edge where there was none before. She thought to straighten it, and stars exploded above her and she gasped.

There was a restrained silence, and then Sett's hand found hers, pulling it gently from her face. Ria shivered again, the wait of the days, the weight of her knowledge piling up like drifts during a storm. She slipped out of the cot and, under the warm wool of the blanket, to where Sett could breathe on the back of her neck, and she could sleep.

Not quite dawn and the birds were strangely silent for a mountain morning in June. Poke blew into the stillness and saw a cloud of his breath in the gray light. The stove must be out. He braced himself to get out of the bedroll and kindle the fire. He sat up and quickly pulled on his boots, then opened the door to the stove with a loud creak. Wincing, he glanced over at the cot, but it was empty. Tinder in hand, he turned for a closer look. Dog was there, same place, and Sett was lying on his side although it was unlikely he was asleep.

"Sett? You awake?" Poke whispered in the icy air. Sett shifted onto his elbow, carefully loosening the girl's long hair so as not to pull it.

"Look outside, Poke. I think it snowed."

Poke turned his back, stuffing the kindling into the firebox and striking the flint more to give himself time than to hurry the heat. He carefully avoided the back of the tiny room as he went to the door. A handful of powdery flakes swirled in as he swung it open.

"How'd you know that?" Poke asked. Sett appeared beside him, fully dressed. Poke assessed the face, neither embarrassed nor contrite. He was having no more luck keeping up with Sett Foster the man than he had with Sett Foster the boy.

"I could smell it," Sett offered.

"I'm surprised you had the time." His own tone surprised him. His cheeks reddened as he realized that he sounded like a fussy old lady. Maybe the stress of the past few days was catching up to him.

"That's between me and the girl."

Poke stuck his face out the door, examining the white world and hiding from his friend.

It was certainly not the first time he had witnessed a June snow, but the scene was always surprising. Several inches of thin white dust covered the new blades of grass and sat weighted on the fresh green leaves of the aspen. The creek bounded along between bell-shaped icicles clinging to the exposed roots on the banks. He pushed the door wider, allowing Sett to step into the strange morning, where domed caps of snow topped the purple of the summer iris. Absorbed into the stillness, they stood and, with the mind of the stockman, thought "good for the grass." Then Poke's face broke with dismay.

"I'll leave a trail bigger than shit, leading right to your door."

"Can't do nothing about that now." Sett paused to study the backtrail, the south slopes which somehow hid Muldoon and Augie, giving no clue yet to their whereabouts. "It covers my tracks, so it all depends on how close they are. Or if they're close at all. You better leave soon, before it melts to mud."

Poke scuffed the powder with his boot toe. "Sett, I owe you an apology."

"That's enough, Poke. After all you've done . . ."

"No. I do, and I guess I owe one to the girl too. She's

a determined one, Sett, hope you're ready for her.''

Sett nodded.

''I want message of you to the post just as soon as you can. Or I'll stew myself with fussing.'' Poke tried to grin, but it came out all lopsided.

Sett's gaze clung to the pale wash of the distant ranges. It was all worth it to see the horizon.

''I'll get your horses.'' He took the first steps into the pristine cover that would only last until noon.

Poke went back into the cabin. The girl was up, feeding sticks into the stove. The bloody shirt was pulled closed with a belt, her hair still tangled, but the bruised eye was slightly open and she stood unaided.

''You look better,'' Poke said when she acknowledged him. He checked the door to make sure they were still alone. ''When the Johnson women get to Verdy, there'll be a posse, of sorts, heading out after Sett.''

''Why?'' she said.

''They're goin' to say he threatened the Johnson women, and kidnapped you. And that he's back to get the gold from the robbery.'' Poke squinted at her. ''You got two days. I'll try to slow them down, but you have got to get Sett out of here. Make him take you over the mountain. Make him stay there. Johnson and Muldoon won't follow that far.'' Poke walked over to the pack saddle and pulled a cloth out of the pannier. He gathered up a handful of Samantha's neatly wrapped bandages and laid them on the cot. He took off his coat, unbuttoned his wool shirt and handed it to Ria. Pulling the coat back on over the cotton Henley, he did his best to return her frank stare, to make her believe what he said. ''Don't tell him what you know. If he knows, he'll stay. And if he stays they'll shoot him before he ever gets a chance to explain.''

"This posse does not care about the mother and the sister, Elizabeth?"

Poke hesitated. He could hear the horses being led out of the aspen. "Look, just keep him alive. I'll deal with that later, but you, get him out of here."

Captain Muldoon had gloves, one of those citified things about him that Augie hated. They had appeared out of the pocket of the long coat, along with other specialized items that Augie had not dreamed of owning, such as the monocular. Now Muldoon was scanning the upper slopes with his warm hands handling the little brass tube while Augie tucked his paws up into his sleeves and hunkered down into his coat. It would be warmer to be moving, and right now Augie was all for heading back down the canyon out of the snow, but the cap'n was taking his time with the examination of the headwaters of the creek.

"Hmmm." Muldoon pursed his thin lips and lowered the glass from his eye. "I think he's in that cabin."

"What cabin? Where?" Augie frowned. Muldoon pointed up at the arched ridge of White Buffalo Mountain.

"See that rocky outcropping? At the edge of the trees?" He put the glass back up to his eye. In the tiny scope, he could make out the open door of the line shack, and the two figures, one tall and one short. They were saddling a horse. It looked like the short man was going to leave. Muldoon kept his thoughts to himself. The tall man had to be Sett Foster, and so likely the other one was that presumptuous storekeeper who ran the post. What was he doing up there?

"Hmmm" escaped his lips.

"What? What do you see?" Augie longed to have a

turn at the spyglass. As many times as he had sat in this position in the army, no one had ever offered him a look through.

"Someone's saddling a horse."

"Do you see my girl?"

"No." A vision of the breed girl crumpled in the grain box flashed in Muldoon's mind, with the idle wonder of whether she was dead. Then he cleared the thought as if clearing his throat. The storekeeper was mounting up. A packhorse was ready behind. Sett Foster stepped back into the dark of the cabin door and disappeared from Muldoon's view, as the mounted man and packhorse started out across the snowy meadow.

"There he goes," Muldoon whispered as if his voice would carry the miles up the mountainside. "He does have your girl. She's tied on the other horse."

Now Augie could see them, black specks angling across the white background. He shoved his hands out of his sleeves and gathered up the reins.

"Let's go. Don't want them to get away!"

"Wait a minute, Johnson. Think about this." Muldoon was wiping off the eyepiece of his glass, watching Augie Johnson's face grow redder with excitement. "They're heading this way. He's probably going in to his friends at the post. You go straight down canyon, wait in the rocks. I'll come in behind and we'll have him trapped."

Augie pondered for a moment. He watched as the black specks entered the trees and disappeared from his view. "Good idea, Cap'n, but I want the first shot at him."

The corner of Muldoon's mouth twitched. "Of course."

*　*　*

"I certainly hope this doesn't slow down the freighter!" Constance Johnson fretted as she peered out the window at the snowy peaks.

"The road winds up the valley. I doubt there's much snow." Abby wished she could judge for herself the depth of the spring frosting. Samantha had not sat to breakfast, tension forcing her to make rounds of the kitchen, stirring, chopping, scraping, stirring. Even little Gail had escaped the tightness of the cabin. She bundled up and went to the barn to start the chores. Abby sat with her knitting in the corner by the stove and listened to Connie Johnson's verbal hand wringing, and her daughter's simpleminded comments.

"I wonder where they are," Carolyn voiced wistfully. "Do you think they're in the snow?"

"I'm sure your father knows how to find shelter," Abby offered.

"No, I meant the outlaw. And Ria." Carolyn swiveled in her chair to watch Samantha measure out a scoop of beans for the soup. "It would be scary, don't you think, Mrs. Miller, to be carried away by a wild man like that? A killer on the run? Maybe he killed her, or worse. But then maybe that's what she deserves for flirting with him like that."

Samantha barely paused as she skimmed the beans through her fingers, checking for pebbles before dumping them into the kettle.

"I wouldn't know," she said through clenched teeth. She pictured Sett's shy grin, the polite thank-you for her cooking and the hurt in his eyes after learning about his family. She remembered her own words—*Any time, Sett*—and truly wished that she too knew where he was and exactly who he was with.

Poke would not freeze to death in this late gasp of

winter; neither would any of the others, all having grown
up in this country and well aware of the pernicious nature of the weather at this high altitude. But it would
slow them down, change the tracking and certainly be a
hindrance if there were any injured. That thought alone
kept Samantha bustling around her kitchen, chopping
dried onions for the soup and fighting the urge to snap
at her self-centered guests.

"At least it was her was carried off. When he sneaked
up on us in the yard, I saw my life go before my eyes,"
Carolyn continued. She patted herself on the chest. "I
was afraid to go to the outhouse alone. Thank goodness
Captain Muldoon talked Papa into sending us here."

Samantha bit her tongue. She and Abby had agreed
for all concerned not to say anything about Sett Foster
and Poke. It was best if these women went on their ways
and did not implicate Poke in Sett's doings, until Poke
did himself. But how hard to not correct their addled
thinking!

Connie turned away from the window and helped herself to another cup of coffee. "Well, I must give the
outlaw credit. At least he availed himself on that little
tramp who wouldn't know the difference and left the
decent women alone." She checked to see that the children were not in the room and went on. "Everything
they say about Injuns is true. Sluts and murderers, all.
Sleep with anybody. Steal your husband, wear animal
skins and no proper undergarments! Born whores."

Mother Abby dropped her knitting in her lap. "That
girl is just a child. A child! And brought out to the
homestead by your husband, Mrs. Johnson!" Samantha
froze in her tracks at Abby's words. She had not been
the only one pinching back the truth. Connie sputtered
on a mouthful of coffee.

"Why! Whatever are you implying?"

Abby stared at her with her milky eyes. Her lined face was composed, anger showing only in the line of her thin lips. "Only that I wouldn't bring up the subject of immorality, were I you."

Carolyn broke in indignantly. "Ria went to the outlaw's camp. She was keeping time with him."

"Best to not discuss Sett Foster, either," Abby snapped.

Samantha held her breath. Her mother-in-law seldom lost her temper, but she also seldom lost a battle. And when it came to defending her family—and most certainly the son of her dearest friend was considered family—Abby would burn these two to the ground. Samantha watched the stillness of the women in the room. She could think of nothing to say to break the spell, nothing to avoid the spilling of the truth, and when the story got to the vigilante committee in Verdy, Poke would be allied with Sett, the Boy Stage Robber back to retrieve his gold.

FIFTEEN

He watched Poke ride down the open meadow and into the trees. The bright edge of the sun was tipping the rimrocks above the line cabin, turning the fine ice crystals to eye-dazzling sparkles, but doing nothing yet to warm the alpine air. Sett stood, coatless, surveying the world below his perch on the arched ridge of the divide. His gaze focused on the yonder, the distant roll of mountain ranges this morning tinted white instead of yesterday's greens and grays. He took a deep breath, drawing in all the space and holding it for fortification.

Poke needed to head for home, to see for himself that all was well with his family, but Sett had no illusions that Muldoon and Johnson were anywhere but on his trail. They wanted the gold. Their determination was somewhat surprising, as if the stakes in the matter were becoming personal. Certainly, Sett took it personally.

They were out there somewhere.

He could elude them, but not with the injured girl in tow. So he was stuck here, or at least nearby, unless he wanted to abandon the girl, and he did not seriously consider that. If Poke were right, and a vigilante posse was soon on its way, it would only be a question of time before defending himself somehow became a demand, and not an option. Sett sighed, and checked the south slope again.

Not that he had any answers, yet. The desperate optimism with which he had ridden back into the Cottonwoods was gone, destroyed by strangers, rumors and five wooden grave markers in the church clearing. Questions still hung in the crisp mountain air, questions to nag him to his own grave. His mother and his sister—their murderers were still walking the world. And the gold, hidden from everyone including him. And the rumors. How far would he have to go to outrun the fables that followed him like unwanted puppies?

Sett took another deep breath of the wild mountain air. The sun was full up now, casting a pale light on the surreal surroundings of snow on fresh greens of spring. In a few hours, the frozen world would turn to a world of mud, the layer of snow melting to bog the creek crossings, and to record the tale of any and all who passed by.

Sett wished he had his makings on him, but they were by his bedroll in the line cabin. A smoke right now would give him an excuse to stay here in the light of morning. To plan the next move. For the next move he could not avoid.

The girl was in the cabin. He could sense her movements. She would not go away, and maybe she should not. She had problems, and maybe they were his all along.

Ria heard him coming in the door and jumped up from her sitting position on the dirt floor, but once up, her vision whirled and she stuck her hand out to balance. The sear of the stove top just grazed her palm as Sett yanked her away.

"What are you doing?" he said incredulously as he sat her on the cot. "You shouldn't even be walking around."

"I made coffee." Ria's skin paled under her tan, the freckles on her nose standing out. Sett scowled at her, then got up and went out. He returned with a handful of snow wrapped in his bandanna, and placed it carefully against her bruised temple.

"You stay in bed, OK? Promise?" Sett paused and shut his eyes. Could he really expect her to follow through on a promise? "Just stay put, so I don't have to worry about you."

"Do not worry about me." She wished her head would stop pounding. The ice felt good, but every small movement caused her vision to blur. "I can go soon."

"Yeah, right." Sett squatted on the floor in front of her, putting himself eye level in her swimmy view. "I need to know who did this."

What was the right answer? What did he need to hear? Ria replayed Poke's warning, and the heated discussion last night. In the haze of her fever, she could remember Poke telling him about the graves, about her wanting to know which one was Elizabeth's. If Sett was listening, then he already knew, but maybe had not realized yet.

Sett tried not to be impatient. Getting a direct answer out of this girl was like pulling teeth. "Ria, answer me. What happened? How'd you get to the homestead?"

The question caught her by surprise. She thought a moment. "I borrowed your friend's horse."

"And tossed my friend in the creek from what I hear tell," Sett stated. "But I meant, why?"

"Coy wanted to go with you. And you know the way over the mountains."

"You went back to the homestead," Sett pointed out.

"I went to get my robe, and some food, for the journey."

Sett appraised her, slender body held straight and still, the cloth with the snow held against the bruise which was shading to purple and black, her hair still in tangled braids with random oats.

"Ria, no one has the right to hurt you. Tell me who did it." Sett leaned over and caught her wrist. He stared into her face, the intensity like a burn.

"The man with the gun." She pointed down with her hand as if grabbing a pistol on her slim hips.

"Him alone?"

She started to shake her head, then thought better of it and said, "Alone."

Sett stood up. He crossed the room in three steps. The girl shifted on the pallet, easing an ache that should not have been there, that she did not deserve. He did not need for her to tell him details; he could see those himself in the swelling of the delicate skin around her eye and the dried blood on the slit poncho.

"Augie Johnson wasn't there?"

"No." Ria waited. She did not want to say too much, to toggle that final conclusion.

He paced once around the tiny room, Ria's eyes tracking his restlessness. She almost winced when his head missed the low rafters by inches, but he didn't seem to notice. His right hand stroked the handle of the skinner on his belt, the other clenching and stretching. He stalled briefly in front of the cot, turned and began a circle back the other way.

Ria thought of the fox in a cage trap she had seen

years ago. It had been caught young and raised by some nephews of First Wife's, and had been in the cage so long that it was no longer terrified, but just circled endlessly with blank haunting eyes. A child, Ria sat by the cage and tried to entice the fox into being her pet, but it ignored her. One afternoon the cousin decided to take the fox out of the cage and lead it around on a thong, like they said the white women did with their dogs. But all that walking had really been planning, and when the boy reached in, the little fox buried sharp teeth in his thumb, and ran, twisting through the tents and fireplaces, his tail flagging until he reached the woods. Ria remembered rolling on the ground with laughter, while the injured cousin shook his hand in pain.

Now Sett was starting another circuit and Ria wondered how many laps it would be before he decided on a course of escape, and wasn't sure if she could stand to sit there watching until then.

Augie Johnson found a place to tie his mule in the side canyon beyond the rocks. He clambered up into the outcropping, carrying his rifle and the extra cartridges from the pack, and settled down behind a stump of a pine that had toppled forward into the creek. He had a brief clear view of the trail across the gravel bed of the stream, and the brambles hid him from any down canyon riders. Augie grunted with satisfaction. He propped the Winchester on the stump and sighted on the trail where it emerged around the bend. An easy shot. He tilted the rifle away, and waited hopefully.

He had never been very good at waiting. With no entertainment, the time stretched long, and he began to imagine what the girl's face would look like when she realized that her wild outlaw was dead and that it was

Augie who'd killed him. Maybe it would be a good thing, bring her back to the respectful girl he'd purchased instead of the way she'd been lately—always staring at him with reproachful eyes. Maybe, if the cap'n wasn't too close behind, he'd take her right there, let her know he was back in control and that she could not slip away again.

Connie and Carolyn were on their way to Verdy. Maybe he should let them stay there. The cabin was a lot more pleasant without them, for sure. Augie considered the implementation of this. Maybe if he just never showed up to claim them?

And what if the gold was in Sett Foster's saddlebags? He'd have to share it with Muldoon, because if he didn't the cap'n would track him to the ends of the earth, and that was not a pretty prospect. No, when he got the gold, he'd split it fairly with the cap'n, just as they'd agreed.

A magpie flew out of the trees across the creek, and Augie tensed to the rifle sights, but nothing appeared on the trail. He sat for a long moment with the gun leveled and his trigger finger twitching, before tilting it back into its resting position. The snow had been lighter at this lower elevation, but the steep canyon walls still blocked the sun. The chill snapped around him, and he thought about Muldoon's idea of Mexico. There would be lots of sloe-eyed señoritas in Mexico, and his gold coin would go a long way. *I'd be a rich man,* he thought as he sat in the rocks and waited.

From closer up Muldoon could see the smoke seeping out of the stovepipe chimney. The cabin door was open, and a brief flicker of movement showed that someone was inside. He tucked the brass eyeglass back into his pocket and considered the slope.

The melting snow was quickly turning the side hill to slush. His horse slid back halfway on every step. The ridge top might be rockier, better going, but he'd have to turn up now before it got too steep. Muldoon ran a finger along his mustache. Where was the advantage? He did not like the prospect of riding into rifle range of the cabin. Sitting with its back to the bluff, it would be too easy for Sett Foster to defend. Muldoon remembered the frustration of being caught in the meadow camp, with Foster laughing at them from the cliffs. No point in giving him that opportunity again.

Foster had to be watching his backtrail, but it looked like he was going to hole up in the cabin. If he was going to run, he'd have left at dawn, or if he was going into the post, he'd have left with the storekeeper. Muldoon wondered what else was in the hidden cabin, like the gold perhaps? Foster must feel pretty secure here.

Without the monocular, the little cabin blended into the shadows with only the faint smoke marking it. Without that glint of the mirror yesterday afternoon, Muldoon would never have spotted it, and most likely Sett Foster would indeed be sitting there safe. Muldoon reviewed his plan. Some things had worked out, pure luck. The mirror had blinked just at him. Johnson was off down in the canyon waiting for Poke Miller to ride by. Now, if he could just draw Sett Foster out of his hole.

Muldoon's horse was rested, and he urged him along the edge of the trees toward the ridge top.

Coy inched out from under the cot and pricked her ears at the open door. Her nose twitched and she glanced up at Ria, but the girl was leaning back with her eyes closed. The man was still walking, lost in his thoughts. Coy slowly rose, her ruff hair twitched up along her back. Stiff-legged, she drew one lip up and showed her best teeth. Sett froze. He followed the dog's gaze out the door.

"Ria," he whispered. The girl's eyes flew open at the urgency, Now they could hear it, a faint echo of a yell from somewhere down canyon.

Coy let out a low growl. Sett grabbed up his rifle and got as far as the door before he realized that Ria was right behind him.

"Stay out of sight. They don't know you're here. Best if it stays that way." He stepped out and walked cautiously in the shadows of the trees, Coy on his heels.

The stillness of the mountain air was broken by only the birds calling from the willows along the creek. Sett searched the ridges for movement. Coy furrowed her brow, pulling the ears into listening position. She bared her teeth again as a faint voice drifted up from the rocky breaks to the south.

Sett could barely make it out. The caller certainly was making sure to be out of rifle range, and it was not a call for help. It was a man's voice, calling his name.

"Hello. Hello. Foster?"

Sett fought the urge to answer. Did the caller know where he was, or was it just a chance? He focused on the backtrail, on the outcroppings along the creek where the dog was staring.

There. A small movement near the edge of the bluff. He could barely make out a figure on a horse. Sett stood very still, hoping to remain invisible.

"Foster!" The voice sounded sure of itself, and Sett wondered if he had been spotted, and how. He shifted the weight of the rifle in his hands.

"Foster! . . . need . . . talk!" The voice broke up in the

distance and only a few words reached through. "...
information you want . . . talk.''

Sett cursed quietly. He walked out farther into the
meadow, placing himself prominently against the open
backdrop of the wet spring grass. Coy moved with him,
guarding.

"That you, Muldoon?" Sett let his shout carry his
anger down the canyon.

"Yes. Got . . . deal for you.''

"You got nothing I want." Sett lifted the rifle and
sighted on the shifting horseman on the rocks. He could
not hit him from this far, but he fired off a shot anyway,
letting the report echo and watching the man and horse
jump.

". . . not friendly. I know who . . .'' Muldoon's horse
was twirling nervously, the man's words fading and
growing against the walls of the canyon. ". . . your family!''

Sett raised the rifle again, then lowered it. It would
do no good to waste his ammunition in anger. He was
found, and if Muldoon could do it, so could a posse.
There was silence while Muldoon waited for his answer.

"Where's Johnson?" Sett shouted.

". . . alone," the reply drifted back. "Deal . . . tell
you who . . . for the gold. Meet at the cairn!''

"Damn," Sett muttered. He glanced back at the cabin
hidden in the aspen. For sure he did not want Muldoon
to come any closer, to discover that the breed girl was
in the cabin. He checked the doorway, but Ria was
safely out of sight. *If Muldoon doesn't know she's here,
what does he want? Why is he offering information?
How did he find me?* Sett raised a hand to rub his chin,
the stubble scratchy. He turned around.

The shiny square of the trade mirror twinkled from its place on the branch stub.

Muldoon smiled to himself. Through the eyepiece, he watched as the Boy Stage Robber turned back to the secret cabin. He noted the glance at the door, and could read the body language of a perplexed man, one who had thought he was safe and now found differently. He could see him quite well, could see the hand raised to jaw in consternation. Then Muldoon chuckled out loud as Sett Foster stalked over to the trees at the edge of the clearing, savagely yanked down the mirror and flung it against the cabin wall.

SIXTEEN

Poke was glad to be out of the high country and onto drier ground. He pulled the packhorse into a trot and they made good time on the easy grade of the canyon. They would be out in the sun soon, nearing the homestead.

The farther he was toward home, the more his thoughts dragged back to Sett and the girl, up at the cabin. Now it seemed damned unlikely that Johnson or Muldoon was at the post. They had to be looking for Sett. But it had been time to leave, he lectured himself. There was no more he could do there.

He had something to do though, and that was get back to the post and delay the posse, give Sett some time to settle his business and run. Poke clucked up the horses.

The canyon was narrow at this point, both walls thickly forested and the creek rushing along a bed of boulders. It was familiar enough. Poke had traveled up the canyon several times over the years, mostly as a boy with Sett and his father. There should be a tributary coming in soon, and a little flat meadow just below a stand of rocks.

Awareness of the movement happened in the instant of the boom. Poke's mount shied and he dove for his rifle in the scabbard just as the impact hit. The packhorse pulled back in fear, the saddle horse stumbled and Poke rolled off and kept rolling down the creek bank to rest in the berries.

The panicked horses fled down the canyon, and Poke watched them disappear toward home. He gasped for breath, the sound of his own labored breathing blocking everything else. He could see up to the trail, and into the patch of sky that showed above the canyon.

What the hell is going on? He slowed his breathing and tried to move his arm. It seemed to work. It didn't even hurt, but blood was soaking his shirt and he realized he'd been shot. Now he watched the space above carefully, and listened. He figured the shooter was waiting to see if he moved, or trying to figure out where he had landed.

The Winchester was in his right hand. He must have taken it when he fell. Poke pushed himself up on one elbow. Still no sign of the ambusher. Poke would have liked to see him. A sense of injustice filled him. Who had shot at him? And why? He sat up, rested the gun on his knees and waited.

Silence was broken by a scrambling on the bank behind him. The dirty bastard who'd ambushed him was finally getting up the courage to check out his job. Poke brought the rifle up with both hands, the wound still numb and the blood slowing. Poke's vision was red. He sighted on the trail where his assailant would appear.

August Johnson, in his slouchy hat and lumpy coat, tiptoed into sight. He held his rifle uncocked and down, and peered into the shadows of the trees, searching. In his excitement, he'd fired too soon. And now he'd lost sight of the man he'd shot. And he was not even sure he'd shot the right man.

Johnson's confusion showed. Poke wondered where Muldoon was. He waited until Augie turned his back to look down at the tracks, and then drew back the hammer.

Augie spun around and tried to bring his gun up, but froze. His face registered disbelief, and he stared at Poke as if the seated man had horns growing out of his head.

"What? . . . How'd? . . . Where's my girl?" he finally sputtered.

Poke whispered, "Put the gun down, Johnson." Augie heard the coldness in his voice, and complied, laying the rifle on the bank and stepping back away from it.

"You wasn't who I was expecting. It was an accident. There's no need . . ."

"Who were you expecting?" Poke said. Johnson glanced nervously up the canyon.

"The Boy Stage Robber will be along here soon." Johnson pictured himself caught between Poke Miller and Sett Foster, and no sign of Muldoon. He wished he had waited for the man to clear the trees before he'd fired.

"And that's who you were going to shoot in the back?"

"Well, I was going to get my girl back." Johnson fidgeted. "And the gold. And I was goin' to kill him before he killed me."

"Well, I got news for you, Mr. Johnson. Sett Foster isn't coming down this trail. You ain't getting the girl back, and there isn't any gold. And you're going to be sorry you didn't kill me." The pain from his wound now throbbed into Poke's awareness. He pushed it aside, and continued. "Just to satisfy my curiosity as to how low a form of critter you are, Johnson, tell me. Were you watching when your buddy Muldoon raped the little girl and hit her in the head? Or did you help?"

As if shocked, August Johnson straightened up. He stared at the trader from the post with his mouth hanging open. Muldoon had been right; Foster knew about the raid, knew that Augie had been there. He had told Miller. Now Augie's mind did its slow whirl and he blurted, "I didn't kill none of them! Cap'n was in charge of that. I . . . I saw the girl. But I didn't kill her. Or the old woman."

Poke's eyes narrowed. Through the gathering mist of pain, the slip was crystal clear. Johnson was as guileless, and as guilty, as he suspected.

The horses would return to the post, and someone would come out looking, probably Samantha. But that could take a day. He considered the big man standing in front of his rifle muzzle. There would be a certain satisfaction to killing him. Poke had no doubt that he deserved it. But there was a certain use for him too.

"Stand still, Mr. Johnson. Thanks to you I'm not going anyplace soon. And neither are you." He focused on the man's right knee, and squeezed the trigger.

Sett shoved the door open and stormed into the tiny room. The girl was gone, no sign of her. He noticed her bundle and blanket on the cot. Coy went ahead into the room and then sat, looking around.

"Ria? Damn it, Ria, where are you!" He stepped on in. There was a noise, and Sett swung the door closed. Ria was standing behind the door, holding a chunk of firewood. Her eyes were wet, as if about to cry, and Sett glanced at her weapon and back at her face.

"Who were you going to conk with that?" he asked sternly.

Ria dropped the limb. "I did not know who was coming in."

Guilt crept up on him. Here she was, in tears, ready to defend herself, and he was yelling at her. There was a place to send this anger, and it was not toward this injured wild thing. He consciously softened his voice.

"Muldoon is a long ways off, but we're not going to waste time. Can you saddle the big mare?" He looked at her small frame. "I'll do it before I go. Now, you wait awhile after I'm gone, then you take the mare out the back and through the trees. Head for the pass." Sett was collecting his gear, separating items into piles for each of them. He tossed the supply saddlebags into Ria's pile.

"I do not know the way over the pass," Ria protested.

"I've never been all the way over myself, but Talking Crow showed the landmarks to me. You can find them."

Ria's good eye flew open. She jerked her head up to gaze at Sett. "Talking Crow is my grandfather." Now Sett was startled.

"Your grandfather? Why didn't you say something?"

"I do not know." Ria paused, struggling to frame her words. "I never see him. My mother married away." Sett returned to his packing.

"Well, he will take you in. Talking Crow is a good man. You must go up to the top of the pass and look north. You'll see two branches of the Tenderfoot. It's a long way, but follow the right-hand river," Sett demonstrated with a gesture, "until you get to the lake. Go around the sunrise side of the lake, and the camp is under a tall bluff."

"He is your friend. You can go with me," Ria insisted. "Grandfather is a great warrior. He will hide us from the gun-man."

"No, I have to go back. There's business that needs attending."

"Then I will go with you."

"No, you will not go with me. You will take the mare and go over the pass. Muldoon doesn't know you're here, but he could show up here looking for the gold. Even if he does, he'll never catch up to the mare. You go fast over the pass to your grandfather's people." Sett wrapped his possessions in his slicker and started to get his saddle. Ria stared at him unblinkingly.

"The gun-man will only come here because he killed you."

"I suppose so."

"He will tell you lies." Desperation colored her voice.

"Well, no one tells the truth." Sett tossed the saddle up on the extra horse. He girthed up loosely and turned to wipe off the mare's back. "Even you. You won't answer a direct question."

"I do not know the right answer."

"Let me decide that." He finished saddling the mare. "It doesn't matter anymore whether Augie knows who killed my family. Or if Muldoon has information to trade for gold. Or if you know something about Elizabeth." Sett came over to Ria by the door, and took his hat from the peg. He reached out, cupped her face in his hand and traced the edge of the bruise with his thumb. "This has gone too far. That I can see with my own eyes."

She stood back from the door and watched him lead the horse into the meadow. He tightened the girth, checked the bridle and stepped up. Coy whined and Ria kneeled down and held her with one arm. The fine bay mare snuffed quietly from her stall. She too was watching as Sett headed the horse across the iris-studded pasture without a backward glance.

His mounted figure disappeared into the draw where the creek began its headlong rush and then could be seen angling up the far slope. He never once turned, never once looked back, only rode with great purpose toward the cairn at the forks of the stream. In Ria's last sight of him, he and the horse were outlined on the crest of the ridge before they dropped down into the next coolie.

Coy relaxed her tense ears and looked up at her girl.

"Yes, I know," Ria said to the dog. She stood slowly, still careful to avoid the whirling dizziness from the fast motion, and got her bundle. From the belt pouch, she retrieved the carved comb and bag of hair grease, and went to work pulling the knots from her hair. The quiet of the little cabin surrounded her like a cocoon, the late morning air outside still. The distant rushing of the creek and the jays in the willows along the banks reached in faintly, and the breathing of the horse and the dog matched her own. She paused when the final tangle was slicked away. She held up a lock of hair, burnished instead of the ebony she had so admired of her mother's. She remembered the odd reddish tinge of LaBlanc's hair. She could barely recall sitting on his lap and laughing up at him, a small child in a lodge full of family. But he was French, and not a warrior of the Blackfeet. His memory would not tell her what she had to do next.

She did not remember Talking Crow. Sweetgrass Woman left her family to live with LaBlanc on the shore of the Missoura, and when they visited with First Wife's clan, it was a different branch of the Blackfeet. But Ria could remember the stories; the tales of warrior heroes and the name of her grandfather in the recounting of raids and coups. And she could almost hear the chanting voice of an old one saying, *So he braided his hair, and painted his face, and tied up his pony's tail, and sang his war song, then he went to revenge those that had been killed.*

Ria had no war song, and she wondered if it was wrong for her to even think it, but she hummed those words to herself as she plaited her brown hair into two long braids, and found the tiny bag of ochre in her kit, and ground charcoal from the cold stove to mix with the grease.

When she was ready, she went to put the saddlebags up on the tall mare, and could not reach without looking way up, which caused her head to pound. The heavy saddlebags flopped against the mare's side, and she jumped away in the confines of the stall, the motion knocking Ria back against the wall. She gasped. The mare snorted at her cautiously, her dark eyes wide in the dim light. Ria leaned back against the manger, her vision finally clearing and the waves of nausea fading. This was crazy, this trying to ride the Thoroughbred. Sett had only been thinking how fast she was, and not how large and powerful she was to a small injured woman. Ria considered this, but then she climbed into the manger. Sett Foster had given her the horse; if he thought she could ride it, then she could.

Balancing on the rickety poles, she hoisted the saddlebags high enough to clear the back of the saddle and tied them on with double knots. She then crawled down and checked the girth, and went back into the cabin to gather the last of her things.

The belt cinched Poke's blue wool shirt at her waist, and held her pouch with the jerky and flint and tinder.

Her knife was in its sheath, her leggings repaired with a thong she had cut from the edge of her robe. Her only decoration was the strips of badger fur tying off her braids, and the three yellow tears painted below each eye, and the three black lines from lower lip to jaw.

The little cabin was empty, its security and warmth a shelter from all outside, but she turned and climbed back into the manger.

The roof of the barn was low, but if she mounted inside and lay down over the saddle, she thought she would fit out of the door. Pulling the mare's head over, she slipped the bit between her teeth and carefully handled the ears the way she had seen Sett do. The manger wood was rotten and it sagged under her moccasins as she tried to get the mare into a position where she could slip into the saddle. All this fussing was making the horse nervous, and she pawed at the bottom of the manger, making it shake.

"Quit. Quit." Ria tried to sound like Sett, but now the mare raised her leg and banged the flimsy wood. Ria made a jump for the saddle as the manger cracked. Her head spun as she clung to the leather and spoke to the mare. Laying low, her face against the black mane, she opened her eyes and saw Coy anxiously looking up at her. The manger fell over, the mare stepping high around the poles that threatened to tangle in her legs, and just before Ria managed to take the reins and send the mare out the door, she saw a strange thing that would not register until much later: under the destroyed manger, a sturdy lockbox with iron hinges.

Coy met her outside in the aspens. Ria sat up and took a firm hold of the reins, and the mare, thankful to be out of the dark barn, settled. Ria waited for her head to slow its throbbing, then she took her bearings.

She did not remember arriving at the cabin, and she had hidden inside the entire time she was there. Now she could see just how camouflaged the stone-and-log building was against the rocky outcropping. She sighted up to the sharp outline of White Buffalo Mountain, then down the creek to where it joined another and wound into the canyon. Above, the creek plunged steeply from the pass. Sett Foster was out of sight, staying covered in the canyons and trees. She was not sure where he had gone, these high breaks being too far for her to have explored on foot from the homestead.

"Coy." The dog looked up at her and Ria flicked her fingers. Coy circled around the cabin, nose to the ground. Her tail stuck straight out as she examined the scents only she could be aware of. Then she struck off down the draw, and Ria did not have to urge the horse to follow.

SEVENTEEN

"I have never been so glad to see Jack Cody coming over the hill," Samantha whispered to Abby.

"Jack is a reliable one, if not godly or clean." Abby gave a little half smile. "I had better go roust Mrs. Johnson. She'll want to pack." Abby turned and tapped her way into the kitchen.

The freight wagon made its way across the plain, its progress slowed by the mud from the previous night's rain. Jack Cody was slumped in the seat, his back aching from spending last night under the wagon in the cold weather. The sight of the post cheered him; Miz Miller always asked him to dinner, and she was the best cook of any on his route. And he always enjoyed visiting with Poke, filling him in on the doings of Verdy and Helena and the other outposts on his bimonthly journey. He sat up as his team dropped down to the river ford, and he paid careful attention to the muddy water as they crossed.

On the porch of the big cabin, a group of women gathered. Jack Cody squinted. Poor old Poke was always overrun with womenfolk, but this time there were extras. And no sign of the men. The sight caused him pause.

He had barely stopped the team in the yard when a blond woman, closely followed by her younger version, hurried toward him.

"Are you the freighter going to Verdy? We are in desperate need of a ride!"

"Yes, we must hurry. We must get to the sheriff right away," the younger one tossed in over her mother's shoulder. Jack Cody stared at them. Then he craned his neck to look questioningly at Samantha and Abby on the porch.

" 'Lo , Miz Millers," he called.

"Hello, Mr. Cody. Let me introduce Mrs. Johnson and her daughter, Carolyn." Abby's voice was strained, as if holding something back. Jack clambered down from his seat and stretched, still eyeing the strange women. Mrs. Johnson grabbed his sleeve.

"Now, we must go to Verdy. Do you have room? We can pay you." Constance Johnson did not like being ignored, and this dirty freighter was casually walking around her to unhook his team. She and her daughter followed as he led the harnessed pair to the big trough, and tied them so that they could drink.

"Sir! I demand an answer! It is a matter of life or death! Can you take us?" Connie glanced quickly behind her to the Miller women on the porch. They stood there silently, the disapproval a palpable tang in the air of the yard. No help from that quarter at all, and since that morning all Connie could do was wish to be back in a civilized town where the folks had civil alliances. Everyone out here on this wild frontier was an outlaw, or Indian, or a friend of one. She tried again with Jack Cody.

"There is a dangerous outlaw on the loose, and Mr. Miller is away hunting. We are begging your assistance!" The daughter behind her nodded vigorously.

Jack Cody pulled off his hat and rubbed his forehead with meaty fingers. He took a deep breath and stared at the flustered woman.

"Well, ma'am, I can take you into Verdy, but I can't hurry. The team's got to rest, and I got to unload the Millers' supplies. It's hard going in this mud." He pushed the hat back onto his head, and looked again at Samantha Miller. Something strange going on here, and he wondered where Poke really was.

Samantha read his hesitation. She called, "Please come in to supper, Mr. Cody. I have a nice stew ready."

"Thank you, Miz Miller. I been looking forward to that all the way from Token's hotel. I'll tell you, they can't hire a cook to save a life." He gratefully walked away from the annoying woman and headed for the house. Poke's eldest daughter came out carrying a kettle of steaming water, and Mother Abby met him at the bottom of the steps.

"I'll show you where to wash," she said, and Jack Cody knew right then that something was really wrong, because he had used the washstand at the side of the house every time he'd been here for the last two and a half years. There was a snort of exasperation from the Johnson woman, and she called after him.

"This is an emergency! There's not time to eat and gossip!" And she planted her fists firmly on her ample hips.

• • •

"Where'd them two come from?" Jack Cody asked as he splashed hot water on his face. He scrubbed futilely at the grime on his neck.

"They're the ones from the old Foster homestead, the ones who showed up a few months ago." Abby held out a sacking cloth for a towel. "They've been here since yesterday." Jack Cody nodded. He remembered Poke telling him when they came through, two city women joining reclusive old August Johnson and his squaw. They had shared a laugh in speculation of that meeting.

"Run in with an outlaw, they say?"

"Yes, but I don't believe they are in any danger."

"Really?" Jack Cody considered Abby Miller. She had lived her whole life in the wild places, and he admired her sense and judgment. She saw a lot more with her cloudy eyes than women like Mrs. Johnson would ever see with both eyes wide. "Where's Poke?"

Abby's face turned worried. "He left yesterday morning to find out what was going on. He hasn't come back yet." Her gaze drifted off to the Cottonwoods, the mountains filling the distance in her mind. "I'm not sure where he is, or who he's with."

The smell of the stew teased Jack Cody's nostrils. His stomach rumbled, but his curiosity held him.

"Who he's with?"

"A few days ago, August Johnson came by with another man, a gunman called Muldoon. And a day before that, we had a visit from an old friend. And those two," Abby tilted her head toward the house, "say Poke's friend is the outlaw, and that he kidnapped the little Indian girl that Johnson kept. But that is not what Poke believed, nor do I." Abby focused her sightless eyes on the blurry form of the freighter. "All I am asking of you, Mr. Cody, is not to believe everything they say, and not to send the vigilante posse out from Verdy. Give Poke time to settle this.''

Jack Cody narrowed his eyes. There must be a lot she wasn't telling him, but maybe her reasons were valid. He had not been in this country all that long, and he, as much as anyone who came to this remote wilderness, had history that he'd rather leave behind. But he had heard the stories, the legends.

''You think Poke is with his outlaw friend?''

''His friend is not an outlaw.''

Jack Cody appraised the small woman in front of him. ''I think you are a brave woman, Miz Miller. You open your home to strangers, and defend the reputation of dangerous men.''

The smell of supper made his mouth water, and Jack Cody clumped on into the room and sat in his usual place to the right of the head of the table.

''Please, Mr. Cody, as the man of the house at the time, sit in the chair.'' Samantha indicated the crude straight-back chair where Poke usually sat. Cody stood, embarrassed, and reseated himself, then he rose again and removed his hat and hung it on the peg by the door. Samantha placed a bowl of stew on the table, and took her seat opposite him. Mrs. Johnson and her daughter sat on one side, Mother Abby and Gail on the other with the toddler, having already been fed, playing quietly on the floor behind them. An uncomfortable silence filled the cabin, competing with the thick scent of elk chunks simmered with last year's potatoes and dried onions. Jack Cody wondered if he was supposed to pray or something, and he swallowed loudly.

"Please, go ahead." Samantha handed the bread basket to Connie.

"No grace?" the woman asked in a voice dripping sarcasm, and she helped herself to two slices of bread. Jack Cody spooned up a big portion of the stew, and blew on it to cool it, while waiting for the bread to reach his end of the table. Nothing as unpleasant as a gaggle of warring women, he thought, and then he immersed himself in Samantha's good cooking and tried not to think about it. That did not last long.

"How long will it take to reach Verdy, Mr. Cody?" The Johnson daughter—what was her name? Carolyn?— was gazing at him with big blue eyes. Jack Cody had just started chewing on a big chunk of meat, and he tried to hurry before mumbling his answer.

"Oh . . . we should be there . . . tomorrow night?" He swallowed. "Barring getting stuck in the mud."

Connie Johnson looked perturbed. "That's as fast as we can go? What if we left the heavy cargo here?"

"Nah, I got to deliver my shipment. Won't get paid if I don't," Cody protested.

"Is it a big shipment? I mean, is it worth a lot of money?" Carolyn opened her eyes wider, leaving Jack Cody caught in her gaze.

Her mother broke in. "If we leave now, where will we spend the night?"

Jack Cody never took his eyes off the younger woman. She had her mother's broad nose, and her raw-boned height, but her golden hair was trailing down across her bosom, and a mighty fine bosom it appeared to be. Jack spooned another chunk of Samantha's stew into his mouth and chewed heartily. Then he remembered the mother's question.

"Well, I sleep under the wagon. But we could fix up a bed in the wagon for you womenfolk."

"Is that safe?" Connie said.

"With a man like Mr. Cody under the wagon, how could it not be safe?" Carolyn asked her mother, while watching Cody blush.

Abby reached under the table, and pinched Samantha's knee. Her face remained neutral, and she sipped at the cup of coffee that Samantha had carefully placed in the usual position off the edge of her plate.

Young Gail, sitting next to her grandmother and facing the door, was the first to notice, but Mrs. Johnson was sputtering away and it was not nice to interrupt. Gail opened her mouth to tell, but Carolyn blathered on in, some inane remark about safety, so Gail once again closed her mouth. Finally, she leaned over to Mother Abby's ear and whispered.

"There's horses coming in."

Samantha rose quickly and went to the porch. There was a dark spot of movement on the distant slope of the foothills. Abby and Gail came out to stand beside her, and Jack Cody peered out the door just long enough to see how far away it was and then returned to his meal. Gail strained her young eyes to make out what the spot in the distance was. She could not tell. In the distance, all she could make out was the movement on the trail; no wagon or horse count.

"Who is it?" Abby asked in frustration at the silence.

"I don't know," Samantha said.

"They're going fast, then slow, then fast again," Gail informed her grandmother.

"Let's return to our guests," Samantha tried to sound unconcerned, "and keep a watch. They may not even be coming here."

"May I eat out here?" Gail checked hopefully with her mother. Samantha nodded.

"So," Connie interjected as Samantha sat down, "more customers?"

"I don't know. Whoever it is, is too far off. And it could be Indians or cowboys who will ride right by."

Carolyn squeaked, "And it could be the Boy Stage Robber." Jack Cody caught Samantha's eye, saying nothing as he mopped up the last of the stew with his bread crust.

"Perhaps it is Mr. Miller returning from his hunting trip," Connie sneered.

"Perhaps it is Mr. Johnson, coming to say all is well and that you can safely return to your homestead," Abby snapped back. She wished she could hurry Jack Cody down the road with these two, but that wouldn't be prudent.

"Mama," Gail called from outside," they are coming in fast now."

This time Jack Cody was the first out the door. He walked out to his wagon, and pulled the shotgun from under the seat. Sounded like there were plenty of potential visitors, only one of whom he trusted. The incoming horses could be seen now and he was trying to decide if his eyes were playing tricks on him in the light. There were no riders.

"It's Roanie!" Gail cried. And the sturdy roan gelding nickered at the sight of home, and pulled the reluctant packhorse toward the ford.

Poke drank from his cupped hand, and wiped the dampness across his forehead, and glanced up the bank. His shoulder throbbed, and he grimly considered the effort of climbing back up to the trail where he'd left August

Johnson. Not that he had much choice. He had better try
to start a fire, gather wood, in case the horses took their
time getting home and night fell. His supplies had gone
down the canyon with the packhorse, and Johnson's
mule must be tied up in the trees, but he hadn't the
energy to go looking for it. Johnson was no help now.
He lay moaning against the bank after Poke had tied up
the wound. He probably wouldn't die. At least not if
help got here soon.

Poke wet his bandanna in the creek and carried it up.

"Here, Johnson." He tossed the soggy rag on to the
man's face. Johnson sputtered, groaned loudly and
cursed.

"Why didn't you just kill me and get it over with?"

"Too easy. 'Sides, you got something to say to the
sheriff, don't you?" Poke gathered some tinder from
under the pines and scraped away the duff with his boot
toe. Each movement was painful, and he was awkward
with his arm held to his chest. He thought about the last
of the bandages, now on their way back to the post in
the saddlebags. Thankfully, his knife was on his belt,
and the flint he always carried in his trouser pocket. He
kneeled down to start the fire.

"Johnson, how far away is your mule? Is your roll
on there?" No answer. Poke flicked a pebble at him, but
the man only shifted his good leg. Poke fed sticks to the
flickery fire, checked the progress of the sun across the
blue patch of sky and wished he had a cup of strong
coffee.

He watched down the trail, knowing full well that no
one would be coming from the post this soon. He was
not worried about Muldoon showing up either. Johnson,
for all his hollering when Poke had wrapped up what
was left of his knee, had been feeling guilty enough to

give his side of the story. Insist though he did that Muldoon was right behind them, Poke knew a setup when he saw one. Which meant that Muldoon was closing in on Sett and the girl by now. And there was not a goddamned thing he could do about it.

EIGHTEEN

When do you go kill a man? When you find out you were grieved, or when you know you'll come to grief? Sett did not hurry the horse down the canyon. There was still plenty of daylight left, the sun shining brightly down and the morning's slush already dry on the thin dirt over the rocks. Sett let the horse pick his way. For once he felt grounded in the present, the facts and matters of the past laid out for examination. In the clear day, with a clear head, he sorted through his options.

Maybe it was best to believe Poke—that it was too risky to stay around and avenge his family. That could wait for another day, perhaps more to his advantage. They had been dead for years, and he had nothing better to do. He could follow the girl over the mountain, stay with her or go on his way. He could postpone this way for years, or until he convinced himself that the killers must be dead and there was no further reason to carry the grudge. That was one way of avoiding it.

Not a good way. There were too many wasted years already in his kit. Of course they could have been no years at all. When he'd stood in front of Judge Carlyle with Whitey and the others, he fully expected to be sentenced to hang. He hadn't even heard the judge read the sentence for them, until the man addressed him.

"Young Mr. Foster, you have made some very poor choices, and now you are going to pay for some of them. Your involvement in this makes you an accomplice of murder, but you were not present, nor did you plan it. In consideration that you did not decide to take a life, I have decided not to sentence you to death. Ten years in the Territorial Prison."

A terrible confusion had followed. Sett could not remember feeling relieved, or guilty or lucky, just lost. He sat overnight in the cell, where Whitey, Jed and the Tejano had smoked and talked in low voices, no one sleeping. No one spoke to him until dawn.

"Boy," Whitey said quietly across the small space, "you 'member you said you always wanted to homestead that little line cabin, the one we stayed in?" Sett had nodded, wondering why Whitey cared about this. "Well, you go back home there and do that, OK?" Whitey had stared into Sett's bleary eyes, his blue ones as piercing as icicles. When he got no response from the exhausted boy, he repeated, "You go back there when you get out, fix up the cabin."

Sett shook off that dark memory and breathed deeply of the sage-scented air. That was another option, with its own price. To have the courage enough to stay, to defend his home, to live on the land of his birthright. For this he would have to kill men.

He pulled up on the next hilltop, and stayed hidden in the trees, while the horse rested and he rolled a cigarette. The creek forks joined below, still far enough away that the twisting line of willows and brambles that

marked their courses was just thick green yarn across a
rumple of paler cloth. He steered his mind to more prac-
tical matters. Why had Muldoon wanted to meet at the
cairn? He visualized the location, the cairn a tower of
rock built from the flat plates of stone that flaked off the
rimrocks. It sat open and vulnerable on the point of land
that divided the watershed into its north and west
branches. There was no approach from the west; the rimrocks dropped off in a steep crumbling cliff. No place
for an ambush, and that seemed most likely considering
his previous encounter with Muldoon.

Sett hunkered down under the shelter of the pines and
finished the cigarette. He could see no strategic advantage to Muldoon's choice of meeting place, other than
that they both knew where it was. Maybe the gunman
really intended to just talk, to exchange information.
Could Sett just shoot him, using the advantage of the
rifle over the pistols? Sett crumbled the cold ashes of
the cigarette butt and cast them to the wind. What information could Muldoon have about his family, information that wasn't lies and that outweighed what Sett
knew about the man and his cruel ways?

There were no ghosts in the trees this morning, his
family quiet for once in his head, but the image of Ria's
battered face was as clear as the crisp edge of the horizon. Her bones would heal a little skewed, to remind
him every time he looked at her, the price she had paid
for association with him. Sett felt the odd nagging again,
as if he had forgotten to tell the girl something important. Then he wondered why he was worried about looking at her; he might not ever see her again. Unless he
turned right now and headed after her over the hills, he
would be where? Down there? Sett stood and took up
his reins.

He kept the horse in the cover of the trees, or the rocky bluffs. Muldoon would be at the cairn marker by now, waiting for him, baiting him. Sett allowed himself to imagine his hands on the man's throat, the blade of the skinner pressed against the flesh. He imagined telling Muldoon exactly why he was going to kill him, and then doing it.

The country was unfamiliar and Ria glanced back often to take her bearings from the peak of the mountain and the landmarks along the trail. She wanted to be able to find the cabin again if she needed, but it was as much habit to observe her surroundings. The Thoroughbred mare moved smoothly after Coy, needing no guidance and negotiating the boulders and muddy spots, giving Ria space to mull the countryside. The gun-man was someplace by a cairn, and she had never heard Augie mention one, but a marker would not be unusual on a trail over the pass. There could even be several. She was thankful that Coy was leading the way. Occasionally Ria spotted tracks from Sett's horse, but where he seemed to be going carefully in the shadows of the trees, Coy cut across the headwash of the coolies to pick up his trail on the other side. At this rate, she could overtake him, but then she would not know where to go.

The mare took a long step into the next grassy depression and Ria reined her up and whistled for her dog. Coy returned, but paced restlessly around as Ria sipped some water from the water bag. She did not want to blunder into something. She did not know the land, but she did know the gun-man, and he would not be casual about any meeting. She must be watchful, and hidden. She must take the time to see.

She could not yet join up with Sett; he would only

send her away, or take the mare, or otherwise prevent her from going with him. Ria took another drink, the water cold and rekindling the throb in her head. She could see out of the black eye, but the swelling blocked peripheral vision. She made an effort to swing a casting gaze in all directions.

No sight of Sett, nor of any other living creature save the birds. Midday, the grazers were holed up in the brush and the stalkers were sleeping off their morning's kill. And the few that might be out, had been scared off by the travel of men in an area that saw few. Ria wondered if Sett would look back, to see if she was following him. She wondered if Augie, wherever he was, was looking for her. She wondered if Muldoon thought her dead.

Coy was eager to be off, and she would run until she found Sett, with no hesitation to timing. When Ria motioned the mare, she took off, until Ria's whistle called her back. Ria guided her party into the trees, moving, as rapidly as the cover would allow.

Coy alerted her to Sett's horse, the figure dark under trees on a bluff below. Ria pulled up quickly, and dropped behind the ridge again to tie up the mare. She kept a close eye on the blue bitch, afraid she would decide to join the man and horse, but Coy sensed her concern and lay tensely at her side. They could not see Sett, and Ria assumed he was doing exactly what she was: spying down on someone.

There was a treeless bench below the rocks, and the two forks of the creek met below it to begin the steep journey through Buffalo Canyon. One side of the flat top sloped to the North Fork, its banks lined with heavy brush. The other side, along the west fork they had generally been following, dropped off steeply, with crumbling rimrocks and shale slides hiding the actual creek from view. On the promontory above the forks was the cairn.

Ria listened carefully: a few jays and some bush tits just above her in scrub brush, and far away the roaring of the west fork in its stony canyon. She took a deep breath, though it reawakened her pounding temple, then she did it again. She looked at Coy, wished for her keen senses. The dog stared out and glanced side to side as if monitoring the situation. Ria was sure now. She smelled wood smoke. Someone had a campfire over the last ridge, and she did not think it was Sett.

For a moment the idea of being close to the gun-man, with his cold grip and even colder eyes, started the beads of perspiration. Ria cringed back from her perch and checked all around. There was no way for him to have seen her, no way for him to sneak up on her, she reminded herself. But still, he was there, and so maybe too was Augie. She grabbed the edge of her panic, turning it away from herself like a blade. She was armed; she had her knife, and her dog, and Sett Foster. The gunman would not scare her away, and she would stay until he was dead.

There was movement near Sett's horse. The tall man slipped down from the trees and Ria watched as he checked his rifle, patted the knife on his belt and reset his hat on his head. He never looked up toward her place in the trees, or back along the line he had just traveled. He adjusted the saddle and mounted the horse, but instead of going directly over the ridge, he turned and rode into the trees, to circle around and approach the clearing from another side.

Ria waited until she was sure he was gone, and then she led the big mare and the dog to where she could take up Sett's lookout in the trees.

The smell of the fire was close now, and Ria crept up to the edge. The gun-man was camped in a jumble of boulders across the grassy table. He was sitting by his fire, sipping at his tin cup. His horse was staked, saddled, close by. There was a small pile of limbs he had hauled for his fire, and his roll was spread out as a seat, but it wasn't a permanent camp. He was just waiting, here in this wide open space, for Sett Foster to show.

The space was a little too wide open for R. J. Muldoon. In fact the longer he sat there by the fire, the more he cursed this location. Without Augie Johnson along, he was lost in the landscape, and the cairn on the backtrail had been picked because it was the only landmark he was sure they both knew. He had placed the rimrock cliff to his back, but that was just old habit. Sett Foster was alone. No one would sneak up behind him.

More to worry about was all the places Foster could appear. The land on all sides was open and easy to traverse, and Muldoon kept a tight watch on the perimeter of his view. He had scanned the breaks above with his eyeglass, but had seen only a small coyote dash across a clearing high up.

Hard to believe that Foster would shoot him from ambush. That was another reason he was sitting out here like a duck on a pond. He wanted to talk to the Boy Stage Robber, he wanted to know where that gold was. He wanted Foster to leave his Winchester in the scabbard and get down to talk to him, because if he could get that far, he had no doubt that the Boy Stage Robber would tell. What came next would be easy. What came next he had practiced many times.

So for Muldoon, crouching by a tiny fire drinking weak coffee out of a cup that burned his lips, it was not

the ending of the story that bothered, but getting through
the beginning.

Again, Sett did not hurry the horse. He traveled quietly,
careful to leave a cushion of distance to dampen any
unexpected sound. He paused often to listen, to think
about the grassy slope and the placement of his enemy:
the rimrocks, and the setting sun eventually, this time
behind the gunman instead of in his eyes. This time no
way to appear without crossing the short spring grass,
no taller than the vivid red heads of the Paintbrush. Sett
suddenly wished he were riding the bay mare. This horse
of Poke's was solid, but the mare had read his mind.
She was taking Ria over the pass to safety; there was
no point in grieving her loss right now. Sett pushed the
thought away.

It would not go away.

That vision of Ria: bruised face with its determined
set; the dark eyes that looked for his honesty; the un-
demanding reason, never asking him to promise.

He could not remember ever seeing her smile.

He stopped the horse.

The pass was hidden by the thickness of the forest,
and the peak of the mountain loomed blue behind the
tops of the trees. Sett turned to it. Was she there, dropping over that divide now and on her way down to the
headwaters of the basin? On her way to her grandfather's
people on the reservation land to the north? Riding
through the wild country alone on his fine big horse,
escaping the slavery that had not dented her heart? Sett
waited. Why was he here, and not riding with her into
that space that was left for him?

For so many years, he had heard the voices, the ghosts in his mind asking questions for which he had no answers, and now they were silent. Now the only voice asking questions was his own.

NINETEEN

He chose to approach from the south end of the rim-rocks, skirting all the way around the green plain and through the creek, finally angling up and breaking into the open at the high stony end near the cairn. The horse was blowing hard from the steep climb up the shale, and he burst over the final rise and into Muldoon's range like an avenging angel.

Muldoon started, then cursed himself for being so jumpy. He remained seated, holding the cup as if holding his hand of cards. Foster wasn't galloping down upon him, just walking the horse carefully across the damp grassland. Everything was fine.

Sett rode with a loose rein, rifle in the scabbard and hat shielding his eyes. Around him stretched the broad wilds of the breaks, the sky meeting the horizon below where the world pivoted slowly on the stone tower of the cairn. Each step in the moist sand of the benchland sucked him down into the earth. Each breath drew him up into the sky. Anger, and fear, and confusion were pulled away, leaving only a wonder at the slowing of the world, and clear vision from outside to in.

He stopped a short ways from Muldoon's fire. The man had not moved. Now Sett could see the gunbelt, with the pistol, hung on the low outcropping which shielded the crude camp from the breezes that blew over the edge of the rimrock.

"What do you want, Muldoon?"

Muldoon looked up slowly, examining up close for the first time the legendary Sett Foster. Mostly legend, from what he could tell. Big and rough, but a loner, one who avoided trouble. And from the description of Johnson's women, very concerned about finding his mother.

"As I said, Foster, I have a deal for you."

"You got nothing I want."

"You want to know who killed your family. You want revenge. You want to get away clean and not go back to prison. I can help you with that." Muldoon sipped at the cup of coffee, conscious of the comforting weight of the derringer in his vest pocket.

"And you want?"

"I want a share of the gold, of course." Muldoon twitched his mouth into his oily smile. "Come on, Foster. I'm unarmed. Get down and have a cup."

Ria's eyes widened. *What is he doing?* She watched Sett swing down off the horse and sit stiffly by the fire, leaving the rifle in the scabbard. She could not hear the conversation, but she could see Sett shake his head when the gun-man offered the coffee, and see the thin man lean back in an exaggerated show of relaxation. He was talking, and Sett was listening and her agitation grew.

Do not believe him, Sett. Now she wished she had worked harder to come up with words in such a way that he would ride away from this, instead of goading him into listening to this snake-man. But she knew it would not have mattered; Sett would have come here anyway.

She wished she had the rifle. It would be so easy. Now she would have to think of some other way.

"Is the gold with you?" Muldoon glanced at the lightly loaded horse. Something seemed wrong about it, but he could not stop to worry over that right now. Foster was quiet, more in control of himself than Muldoon had expected. As a matter of fact, he seemed calm.

"No. I don't haul it around."

"But it's close by?"

"Look, Captain Muldoon. You followed me all this way to tell me your deal. Now do it, before I come up with something better to do." Sett held in his irritation. The butt of the gun hanging on the rock was wiped clean of Ria's blood, but still it called him as if holding a piece of her there. He focused on the thin man's face, the pale eyes emotionless and the corner of his mouth drawn up in a bemused sneer.

"You want to find your family's killer, and he wants to find you, for a different reason. And he has already called a posse. You've got no escape, without me." Muldoon leaned foreword. He dropped another limb on the small fire and waited for a reaction, but there was none. Foster was playing poker, Muldoon thought, and poker was Muldoon's favorite sport. He raised the stakes. "Go take your revenge, head over the mountains. I'll tell the posse I killed you, you'll be free. Why, you can even change your name and come back here to your homestead. I'm sure your friend the storekeeper won't spill the beans."

Sett Foster raised his eyebrows. "All this in exchange for the gold?"

"Simple, isn't it?" Muldoon set his cup down.

"Nothing is simple as that, Captain Muldoon."

Muldoon's eyes narrowed in his long face. He sat up straighter and his hands fell into his lap. Sett Foster was staring at him, the gaze as quiet and steady as the wide blue sky behind him. Muldoon was surprised. Where was the emotion, the gravel of the heart, in the man?

"Of course it's simple, Foster. An eye for an eye. It just takes the doing."

"Yes, good point." Now Sett casually shifted, revealing the skinner in the sheath on his belt. "But my family has been dead a long time, and killing Augie Johnson is not going to spare them, or me, any hurt. Killing you, on the other hand, might." Muldoon had a gun in his vest. There was the slightest flinch toward it as the words struck home.

"What are you talking about? I am here to help you. For a price."

"I'm talking about the girl."

Shock flashed across the gunman's face, then he cleared. "I told you. Johnson was there. He raped the girl, and killed her. Told me so himself, told me how young she was and how white her hair was. Told me they did it in the barn, and left her there when they couldn't find the gold."

Sett Foster was just sitting there, coiled like a snake and staring just as unblinkingly. "The other one," he said.

"The other one? The other one was an old woman. Nothing to do about that. Attacking with an ax." Muldoon shut his mouth. The words rolled like pebbles on the trampled grass between them. Foster did not appear to notice, did not remove his terrible eyes from the face of the gun-man.

"Ria," he said. "I was talking about Ria."

Muldoon dropped his poker face and reached for his gun, but Sett was there on top of him, springing across the fire pit. Muldoon rolled away, tossing himself to one side, scrambling as Sett's blade sliced deeply into his elbow. He groped for the church gun with his left hand. Now Foster crouched, animal eyes measuring the derringer and the blood that quickly turned Muldoon's white sleeve crimson. It pumped, stain growing larger as the men panted.

"Kill me and you'll hang. Is it worth it? The little whore is worth that?" Muldoon held the tiny gun out in front of him, his hand steady. "They're already coming for you. It's not too late. Tell me where the gold is. You can ride away."

"You lying bastard." Sett tried to clear the film from his vision. He was backed up onto the rimrocks, the west fork roaring in the canyon below the rocks, the drop of the cliff only a man's height before the long talus slide and knobby brush fell away to the cold waters.

Muldoon's right arm hung, hamstrung, a dead weight at his side, the blood dripping now onto the lichen-covered plates beneath his feet. He had one shot, and Sett had no doubt he would use it.

Ria grabbed the saddle horn as the nervous mare jigged beside the embankment. She pulled herself into the slick seat and leaned into the motion as the big mare stretched her long legs over the rocky ground. Coy sprinted away, making a beeline through the trees, and the mare followed. Ria ducked the low branches, the image of the men silhouetted on the cliff burned in her mind. They broke onto the bench along the rimrock, the mare clattering across the loose shale and Coy gaining distance as the terrain leveled. Ria thought to whistle her back, but her mouth was too dry from the rushing wind for any sound to reach the flat-back ears of the dog.

The mare never broke stride, her leaps covering rock and limb and the sensation of flying over the treacherous footing leaving the girl's head whirling. She watched the earth rush past, clinging to consciousness as the throb returned, and somewhere in the rushing in her ears, she heard the shot.

One small shot, like the snapping of a twig in the distance.

Ria pulled the mare up, fighting for control against the flight instinct of natural defense. Ahead, the dust rose up to glimmer around the figures on the edge of the rocks. The blue streak of the dog, in slow motion, launched at the arm of the gun-man, knocking him off balance, and Sett Foster rolled back, teetered for a moment as if in indecision, then disappeared over the edge of the cliff.

The first bounce was the hardest, and he rolled with the careening rocks and dirt in a choking landslide, pulling his coat up around his face and tossing himself over the small plants and brush that would have stopped his slide before he was well away. Coming to rest against a sagebrush, he took a deep rattling breath, and squinted out of one eye to see the lay of his land.

There was a knotted pine on the rocks to his left, and the last of the shale loosened by his fall rolled down and settled against it and against his still form. The dust swirled above in the slanting light and he tried to draw his breath and piece together the last seconds.

The dog had come out of nowhere, distracting the gun-man, and latching on to his arm with a flash of canines and the sound of a thousand tigers in her throat. The small gun had fired into space. Now Sett checked each limb for broken bones from the wild descent, but each was whole. He tipped his head slightly, bringing into focus the shale slide and the rough outline of the rimrock shelf above.

No sound. Where was the dog? Where was Muldoon? Where was Ria?

That Ria was there was no illusion. Coy would not have left her, and that she would have followed now seemed a foregone conclusion. Sett cursed himself. She was up on the cliff with Muldoon. And he was a fool.

Muldoon shook the dog off his arm with a yell, and the blue bitch rolled across the tile rocks to land against the foot of the cairn. She sprang back to her feet, teeth bared and lolling tongue extending to tell of her effort. Muldoon glanced at the space where Sett Foster had been, the drifting of the dust telling his trail. He raised the derringer at the dog, and realized he did not have another shot. The pistol still hung in the camp, but the dog was wary, not approaching to attack, and Muldoon grabbed a rock in his left hand and flung it at her. She dodged behind the cairn.

Muldoon snorted through his nose. With great caution, he crawled to the edge of the rimrock, peering down at the settling dust in the canyon and trying to make out where Foster was in the rubble. His right arm was numb, useless from the deep slice through the tendon, and his left now burned where the dog's teeth had slashed. Where had this dog come from? he wondered. He did not recall a dog with Foster.

Below, resting against the scrub of a sage, Foster's body was cloaked in dirt and debris which still bounded down the disturbed slope. No movement. Muldoon waited, his breath still not recovered. The bleeding from his arm was renewed, reminding him of the infliction and making his thoughts reel as he looked over the cliff.

The rocks beneath him shifted, the crumbling edge casting pebbles down upon the still form of Sett Foster.

Do him in. Muldoon's own voice echoed in time to the pumping of his blood.

The boulder beneath him was loose. A shove and it would be hurtling down, carrying with it the rubble of the slope until Foster was covered with the stones of his homeland. Muldoon placed his palm against the rock and pushed. Nothing happened. He tried again, but it was as if his energy had drained. He rested, head tipped forward, until the soft footstep on the stones jerked him. The dog! He had forgotten about the dog!

Captain R. J. Muldoon started to turn, only to see a beaded moccasin settle in the thick blood beside his useless arm. A sharp jab as a knee was planted between his shoulder blades, and a hand knocked off the dusty derby as it grabbed his hair. His last sensation was the coldness of the slice, beginning quickly under one ear and tugging only for a moment at his throat.

TWENTY

The dust was settling, and still he waited. If Muldoon were watching, he would be ready to shoot at the first sign of movement. A few small pebbles cascaded in his wake, and Sett took the time to plan a short move into the pines. As soon as he dared. The roaring of the creek below him drowned out all noise; the red lava shelf above absorbed all sight.

Now there was a motion. The slow tumbling fall of a derby hat. Muldoon's hat. Sett tracked its bobbing descent until it came to rest on the shale. Then he looked back up, and the little merle dog was looking down at him intently. She did not move, except to check once over her shoulder. Sett pushed himself up out of the brush and dirt that had accompanied his fall, and scrambled into the pines.

Limping, he hurried around the boulders and trees at the base of the ledge. Finally he paused, crouched in a sheltered cave and caught his breath. He emptied the dirt out of his boots, and considered going down to the creek for a drink, but did not want to take the time. He had to get back to the top. Sett pulled himself up on a limb and continued around the end of the rimrock to the steep slope above the forks.

The bay mare had drifted down to join the other horses staked in the grass below camp. Coy at first had stared over the cliff where Sett Foster had disappeared, and then she tracked along the rim toward the forks, but Ria did not follow. She released the hair of the gun-man and let his face drop to the shale, then she stepped away from the body and felt the nausea. She wanted to look for Sett, but the dizziness drove her back from the cliff. She leaned against the cairn, willing the whirling and shaking to stop.

She considered the blood on her hands, and the stain where she had wiped the knife on her leggins. She considered the rivulets winding over the flat rocks, the thick smell that rose the bile in her throat. Then she crawled around to the other side of the stone marker and sat, cross-legged, to stare into the distance and regain her balance. She hummed the chant of the old one, the only song of her people she could remember, and waited for her soul to clear.

So he braided his hair, and painted his face, and tied up his pony's tail, and sang his war song; then he went to revenge those that had been killed.

Sett slowed and listened before climbing the last bank onto the rimrock. An eagle was screaming far away, and the stillness of the afternoon air barely rustled the needles of the trees. He pulled himself up.

The horses were in the meadow, his big mare grazing alongside Muldoon's tethered horse. The campfire had gone out, and the bedroll and gunbelt were unmoved.

Sett stayed low in the grass, one knee down in the damp spring earth. There was a rustling, and the little dog met him with a grin and a waving of her tail. Now Sett stood, and Coy turned to lead him back to the cairn.

Ria sat facing him, her eyes unseeing of anything but the long horizon, hands held in her lap. There was yellow and black paint smeared on her face, and the shadow of the cairn darkened the purple bruise around her eye. The dog paused near her girl, then moved away to lie down. Sett lengthened his stride, cautious even in his hurry. Behind the cairn, the motionless figure of Muldoon sprawled in a stain of blood already soaking into the porous gravel of the mountain. Sett knelt down by Ria, but she would not look at him. He stepped over to Muldoon.

A dead man. There was surprise on the gray face. Surprise to actually have it turn out this way.

The morning's clarity returned, and he saw the action taking place as if by actors on a stage. As his own life might pass before his eyes, he saw the breed girl and Muldoon, and he knew why Ria was sitting so still on the other side of the cairn.

He sat down next to her. She was singing to herself. He leaned back against the stones and pulled her into his lap, resting his chin on the crown of her dark head, and circling her thin shoulders with his arms. He thought the repeated refrain was familiar, that he knew it even though he did not understand a single word. The afternoon sun was still high, and as it began its long daily slant, the world in its spinning wobbled a bit as it regained balance.

Poke built up the fire, and occasionally he tossed some green branches on to billow up smoke. The sun had set in the canyon, but it was still dusk and the sky above was light and clear. Poke tried to calculate the hours, and then he hoped that Samantha had not started out alone. His shoulder ached, but he had tied it up with his shirtsleeve, and his coat fended off most of the cold, as long as the fire burned. It would be a long night.

Johnson had rolled closer to the fire, his groans and mutterings fading as he slept. Poke had taken his guns and knives, but now had no fear of the man's ability to fight back. Poke could not even get out of him where the mule was tied.

There was frustration at being so stranded. With the mule, he could start down the canyon, leave Johnson here until he got help. But Poke knew he could not walk even as far as the homestead with the injury to his shoulder. It would be too easy to lose consciousness, or to wander off the trail in the dark and make it impossible for help to find him. Of course, if Roanie didn't go home, he would really be in trouble. Then Poke realized that when he had left, he hadn't been riding Roanie, but looking for him. Would Sam figure out it was he who needed help?

Must be loss of blood, Poke thought. *I can't even think straight. And hunger's not helping.* The last he had eaten was that morning at the line shack.

Then his thoughts skidded. Sett and the girl. What had happened with Sett and the girl? I should have stayed. Johnson wouldn't have had anyone to shoot, and it would have been two to one against Muldoon. Johnson said Muldoon had seen the cabin; that he had looked at it through a spyglass. Poke had an uneasy feeling in his stomach. He wished he knew where the mule was.

It brayed, the odd goose-like call echoing down the canyon. Poke had jumped up, trying to locate the sound, when another sound, a welcome, heartening sound, helloed him from down the trail.

Two riders, with extra horses: one of them the freighter Jack Cody, and the other Poke's own beautiful auburn-haired wife.

The first day of waiting went quickly. Poke listened as Connie Johnson wailed over her poor husband and worried about how he was going to support them with only one leg. They fixed a litter in the freight wagon, tied Augie in and began the jolting journey into Verdy, with Connie sitting in the back by Augie, and Carolyn on the front seat with Jack Cody. Jack carried in his pocket the statement, written in Samantha's neat script and bearing Poke's signature, of how August Johnson had ambushed him for no reason and he had shot in self-defense, and the information of Johnson's part in the murders of Rose and Elizabeth Foster, and their hired man. Poke restrained himself from telling Mrs. Johnson that her husband would hang, so she need not worry about being supported by a one-legged man.

The bustle of their departure left Poke weak, and Samantha insisted he go to bed while she and Mother Abby sat out on the porch with their handwork and watched for riders.

The second day, he sat on the porch, rifle nearby. The late June days were heating up, a hot spell that drove everyone to the cover of the house but for morning and evening, and the chilling drop of temperature at night caused Poke to have nightmares as he wished for some sign of Sett Foster.

The third morning he saddled his horse.

"Poke, you know how I feel about this," Samantha

said again as she handed him the package of meat and bread.

"Tomorrow Jack Cody will be through on the return trip, and he could have a posse with him. I just want to see what I can find out, so I'll know. I won't go far. Be back tonight."

The ride up to the homestead went quickly, in spite of the stiffness of his arm. Only a flesh wound. Poke felt lucky, but then he had always considered himself a lucky man. Still he approached the cabin in the meadow cautiously, noting the tracks in the dusty yard and the dirt on the doorsill. No one had been here.

He turned up the cemetery trail, retracing the steps while replaying the past few days.

Sett could ride away. He'd done it before. In a way, Poke wished he had, this time disappearing to a happier life. In another way, he wanted to see his friend riding in, deciding to stay even if he had to fight. It seemed a shame that Sett Foster had never found a place to stay. For Poke, who had never wandered more than fifty miles from his birthplace, roaming would be a great sadness.

I guess I never understood that look in his eye when we talked about traveling, Poke mused. Sett was always the first one at the storytelling, be it his father's, or a traveler, or the roving bands of Indians that passed through. Maybe he would go over the mountains with the girl, leave Muldoon behind.

Probably not.

As the trail wound up Buffalo Canyon, passing the place of his ambush, Poke's thoughts focused on his surroundings. Logically Muldoon would have left the mountains, either chasing Sett or getting away before a posse showed up. It did not sound like he was prepared to live off the land. Still, each sway of a branch, each darting swallow from the cliffs, grabbed his attention.

The hot spell was unbroken, and by midday Poke reached the head of the canyon and gazed out on the treeless plains of the breaks. He stopped under the shade of the last trees and pulled out some lunch. He could go a ways further, then cut up at the fork and go back to the post by the other trail, making a circuit and still returning home at dusk. There was no sign of any passing, since his in the snowy morning last week. Maybe he would find something on the other side. Poke unwrapped the bread and meat, then chewed thoughtfully and watched the heat of the day send shivers off the rocks into the still air. The creek fork wasn't far, and the bluff dividing it loomed dark over the shaded plunge of the canyon. He loathed leaving the coolness of the forest, and wondered about staying in the creek or going up over the bluff.

Squinting into the bright sky, Poke stopped chewing and folded the remaining food back into its paper. He stood, watched some more and went to his horse. There above the rimrock, the tiny black speck swirled, and descended, and another rose and joined others circling in the crystal sky. Buzzards.

He crossed tracks at the edge of the meadow, but they were days old. He followed them up onto the benchland, and came first upon the campsite, with the cold fire ring and trampled grass. Behind it up on the rocks the tall tower of the cairn marked the ancient way over the pass, and past that at the edge of the cliff the flapping wings and red naked heads of the buzzards. Poke dismounted and climbed up.

The scavengers had been at it, but it was the remains of Muldoon. Poke was sure by the clothes and size, and the bit of hair. He certainly did not want to go closer, especially in the heat of the day.

He did.

No way to tell how Muldoon had died, only that someone had taken his gunbelt, and anything else of value. Poke stepped back, let out his held breath. No tracks on the hard shale. No movement other than buzzards waiting to come back to their find. Sett had not even given him a decent burial.

Poke was not sure if his relief outweighed his consternation. He looked over the cliff. The recent landslide was obvious. What had happened?

Damn him. Poke studied the surrounding mountains. He tried to see the line shack, could only make out the lush green of the grove of trees. Sett could be anywhere.

The cairn stood out against the sky, the familiar stone marker as tall as Poke. Each group passing added a stone, telling how popular a trail was and which direction they traveled. Poke had placed a few stones there himself in times long past, and he grimly wondered if Sett Foster had added a stone before or after he killed Muldoon.

Then he truly wondered.

The top of the cairn was rather flat, and on its circular face there was a stone the size of a man's heart, pointing down the trail through Buffalo Canyon. Going north, two small pebbles, side by side.

TWENTY-ONE

Autumn 1883

Samantha lifted the heavy kettle off the stove, and Poke took it from her quickly. The room was littered with spoons and towels, spatters of preserves on the table and neat rows of jars cooling on the sideboard. Even with the job of canning done, there was still the formidable job of cleaning up. Gail already was collecting the utensils in the washbasin, and Poke carried the hot water outside. He made a mental note to postpone wrapping the water pipe at the trough tomorrow to help with the laundry. Sam shouldn't be lifting that much. Mother Abby helped, and so did Gail, but with a new baby on the way, he worried about the work.

"They're setting nicely," Abby said after an expert tap of her finger on the jar seals.

"There should be plenty, for us and for the customers." Samantha sold her canned goods through the store, certain regulars waiting all year to save a jar of her blackberries for Christmas Eve dessert. Poke admired the jars, today's batch of green beans and beets ready to join the peas and corn on the shelves of the root cellar. They were all ready for the fall busy season, when the surrounding homesteaders would be stocking up for winter. There had been little snow, but the snap of the mornings and the almanac's counting said that they were past the equinox, and the final preparations for the long winter needed to be completed.

Poke carried a box of jars outside, glancing up from habit at the distant road to the Cottonwoods. The hillsides now were tan and gold, the leaves on the canyon's trees a shimmer of red. It was a beautiful fall, Poke thought. *It seems so peaceful. So empty.*

No riders had come down from the hills since the day he took the deputy to see the grave on the rimrock. *Found him out here. No way to say how he died. I buried him decent.* That was as far as he had wanted to go, and the deputy's speculation as to the whereabouts of Sett Foster had brought only a shrug from Poke, and a noncommittal "Could be anywhere."

And that was the truth.

Poke continued on to the cellar and unloaded the jars onto the shelves. Samantha came in to help.

"I guess Jack Cody will be glad these are ready next time he comes through," she commented with a smile.

"Yeah. How that man loves to eat, and he married a girl who can't boil water—I don't know." Poke grinned. Jack's lamentations over the poor quality of his usual meal had increased lately.

"He said he was going to teach her." Samantha rearranged the older jars to make room for the cooling ones. "But I wouldn't want the job of teaching that one anything!"

"Well, at least it sounds like Mrs. Johnson is in de-

mand as a tailor. Jack won't have to support her too."
Poke took the last jars out of his wife's hands. "Funny
thing, those two. I'm glad they're living in Verdy, not
out here."

"Yes, one visit from them was more than enough,"
Samantha agreed. Poke's expression grew somber. She
put her arm around him. "It seems like a long time ago.
It's only been three months."

Poke nodded.

Gail swished the soap in the dishwater, and rubbed it on
the cloth, and was about to plunge her hands into the
hot water when her grandmother felt her way to the
washstand.

"I'll help dry." Abby held out her hand for a towel.

"Thank you, Gramma." Gail put the towel in her
grasp and started in on the sticky spoons.

"It is a pretty day. The sky is so clear and the trees
up on the mountain are turning red and orange. There's
no clouds." Gail began her usual monologue. Mother
Abby relied on her to report the goings-on, and that in-
cluded the weather. "Momma and Daddy just brought
the last batch of beans and beets to the cellar. There's a
flock of blackbirds flying out of the trees behind the
barn, a whole big bunch of them." Gail paused in the
narrative, her hand frozen in the hot dishwater. A man
was riding around the corner of the barn. A man on a
big horse. He looked right at her, grinned and put two
fingers to his lips. Then he reached down and tipped the
latch of the barn door, swung his horse around like she
was a part of his body and disappeared inside, pulling
the door closed behind him. Gail stared at the door with
wide eyes, then she resumed scrubbing.

"Gramma, do you think Sett Foster will come back?"

• • •

Poke helped Samantha up the steep stairs out of the cellar. "I'd better go feed the horses. It gets dark so early now."

"I'll heat some soup," she said, and she headed back to the house.

Poke walked across the yard, lost in thought. Mentioning the Johnson women had called up that whole summer, the unbelievable few days and then the long drawn-out waiting. It was almost familiar, a replay of the boyhood passage, and ripples in life that he knew would smooth out as years went by.

The big barn was on the far side of the yard, the back tucked into the draw that ran down to the river. Its large front door was big enough to drive a wagon in, and each stall inside had a tiny shutter over a slit window. It was the tallest barn in the region, and Poke always felt a rush of pride when he entered. Today, it was followed by bewilderment.

There was a strange horse in the stall. No, it was not strange, he had seen that horse before. Poke froze.

" 'Lo, Poke. Hope you don't mind me staying in your barn tonight, and getting some supplies."

Now Poke could make out the tall man, seated cross-legged on the hay. He was wearing a beaded doeskin shirt, long fringe pooling in the creases, and his hair was tied back with a strip of leather. Dark eyes danced above his thick blond beard.

Poke was speechless.

"Come on, Poke, you look like you've seen a ghost."

"Sett?" Poke sputtered. "You scared the living daylights out of me. What are you doing in here?"

Sett stood up, stretched. "I wasn't sure about riding into the yard. Wasn't sure I'd be welcomed."

"Of course you're welcome." Poke shook his head. "How'd you get in here? You snuck right in here in broad daylight! We were all in the yard!"

Sett grinned. "You and Samantha were in the root cellar a long time. Abby was drying dishes, and your daughter can keep a secret. I rode right around the corner and in the door." He laughed, and Poke was charmed by the familiar sound issuing now from a changed face. The haunted look was gone, replaced with satisfaction. The broad shoulders hung relaxed, his hand on his hip above the sheath knife.

"You look good, old buddy. Where have you been?" Poke was serious.

"Holed up at the line cabin. Actually, got it pretty well patched up. New roof poles. Fixed the stalls. Tight for winter now."

"And Ria?" Poke asked cautiously.

"I couldn't talk her into coming with me this time. I think she was afraid that the Johnsons would still be here. And she is shy of your women."

Poke cocked an eyebrow. "So you didn't go over the pass to the reservation?"

"Maybe next year." Sett stopped smiling. "Thought I'd sit tight unless there was a reason to move." He met Poke's eyes.

"There's no reason."

"You're sure?"

"Yes, I'm sure." Poke turned and scooped grain into a bucket for his horses. "Give your mare a feed."

"Already did." The tone of Sett's voice changed—a hint of the anger, the strangulation of the anxiety. "Poke, where's Johnson?"

Poke stopped halfway to the stalls. He had forgotten the gaps in their knowledge. "Johnson's in the Helena jail. You were right, Sett. He was there when they killed your family. I shot him.'' Poke Miller watched the realization cross the bearded face. ''I don't know if I'd ride into town, were I you, but there's no one after you. You and the girl are away clean.'' Poke finished pouring the grain into the mangers. ''There is something you need to know. I buried Muldoon.''

Sett Foster took a deep breath, held it, and let it out in a slow sigh. He studied the rafters of the loft, the careful placing of the slats, the quickly dying light of the autumn sun.

''Thank you.''

Poke knocked on his own cabin door, then pushed it open.

''Look who's here!'' he announced. Sett ducked through the door. Samantha was motionless by the stove, her shock registered on her face, and the girl, Gail, broke out into a mirror of her father's smile. Sett could not help smiling back, and winking at her. Mother Abby tilted her head to hear better, then pinched Gail's arm.

''It's Mr. Foster,'' the girl whispered, ''and he's wearing *Blackfeet* clothes.''

Sett crossed the room in long steps. ''Hello, Auntie Abby.'' He bent to give her a peck on her wrinkled cheek. Tears ran from her sightless eyes, and she stroked his bearded jaw.

''You are getting ready for winter,'' she teased through her tears, and she could feel the grin spreading across his face.

''Yup. I sure am.''

Abby was sitting near the stove in her rocker.

''I wish you had brought her. I'd like to finally meet

her. Poke told us a great deal about Ria," she said.

"That so?" Sett raised an eyebrow at his friend.

Poke shrugged. "What can I say? She made an impression."

"Especially when you walked home soaking wet," Samantha could not help reminding him.

"Well, more than that." Poke looked at Sett Foster, relaxing by the fire as if he had never been gone. He was the same, and yet not. There was a tempering of the boyish enthusiasm, a cooling of the recent rage.

Now the hazel eyes looked far away, and the voice was low.

"She does that."

TWENTY-TWO

Sett finished the hitch on the new packhorse. The mare was saddled, and fidgeting to be off after her grain the night before. The dawn was clear and cloudless, promising one more day of fall before the onset of winter. Poke snugged his collar around his neck.

"Got everything?"

"I don't think I could fit any more on." Sett slapped a gloved hand on the horse's rump.

"Well, come back. And bring Ria. Ma will never forgive you if you don't."

"Poke, you of all people know I can't make Ria go somewhere she doesn't want to go." Sett chuckled. "But I'll do my best to talk her into it. Now, what do I owe you?"

Poke blushed. "Nah, Sett, don't worry about it. I didn't even write it up." That, he had done for a reason. No point in Samantha finding out how much was loaded on the packhorse, and there was no way he could turn down Sett's requests, even if he never got paid.

"No, really." Sett pulled off his glove and fished

around in the saddlebags. He pulled out a little leather
sack, newly sewn and tied with a thong. From it he
extracted a gold piece, then two more. He dropped the
shiny double eagles into Poke's palm. "That should
cover it." He turned and stepped into the stirrup, swinging up on the tall mare. Waving once to the man standing in the doorway of the soddy store, he let the mare
head out toward the mountains in an easy lope, the laden
packhorse trotting alongside.

Poke looked up from the coins in his hand, and
watched Sett Foster disappear into the folds of the sage-
covered foothills.

Ria fussed around the cabin, sweeping up the floor and
rearranging the shelf behind the stove. She moved
through the space in silence, comfortable in her
thoughts. She'd thought of nothing she needed when Sett
had asked. He had already listed the flour and salt pork,
sugar and beans, and she looked around the room and
thought that they didn't even really need that. She knew
he wanted to see his friend, and she could have gone
with him, but the idea of so many people at once was
disquieting. She chose to remain here.

Coy would have gone. She wanted to follow Sett
when he left. Ria watched her and called her back, until
she settled down on the porch stone in the sun to gaze
mournfully down the breaks.

"You old dog, you are in love with him, I think."
Ria stepped out into the thin sunshine. Fall frosted the
leaves of the quakies to a chrome orange, the thick can-
opy still clinging overhead as if in denial of the approaching winter. It filtered the light into a burnished
gold, and turned the girl's hair brassy. She stood, enjoying the sunlight and the view of the world below.

It was a different view, a view that changed with each passing day and was as old and familiar as it was fresh. Often she stood here with Sett, taking in the horizon in their companionable silence. She also found him here alone, staring off with distant eyes until he noticed her and smiled.

She walked out to the rocky outcropping. The peace that surrounded her now was precious. She did not know how much longer it would last. Maybe that was her reason for not going into the post. She wanted nothing to break this healing calm.

For Sett, it was different. He needed to see the faces of other men and know for sure that there was safety in the soft white months to come. Bruises and cuts healed quickly, compared to lives. Ria reached unconsciously and stroked the eyebrow with its tilted edge. Sett wanted to believe that the calm would stay, that life would pool like the low fall creek, placid as it slipped under the leaves.

She knew better.

This stream would be a raging torrent again in the spring, and an icy trap for the unwary this winter. Until then, she would drift with the season, and let life move along at its own pace.

The gray headboards sat mutely, their carved words no longer a mystery. The brown fall grasses grew thick on the graves; the rattling of the dry milkweed pods chanted in the wind across the knoll. There was a space left for him, his inclusion in death with a family he had abandoned in life. Maybe he would claim that spot someday. Maybe he would not.

Sett slowly read each marker, each name and relation weathering to a memory. He realized he was humming, joining the chanting weeds with words he did not understand but would always be able to recite.

She had sung it so many times over, that by sunset he was mumbling it too, in rhythm with the rocking and the righting of the world. They had slept that night, ate nothing and gathered to leave at sunrise. They never talked about it, never mentioned the memories of sticky blood or cramping gut. Only once he had asked about the song. She had looked at him with that perplexed worry, that she did not know the right answer.

"It says, 'I get ready to go kill him.' "

Not appropriate, Sett thought, and he stopped humming abruptly. Then, he pulled his hat down. The grave markers waited silently, waited for him to go running off again, waited for him to leave them in their rest. Sett decided to tell them, and he resumed his chanting, to sing in the choked words of Ria's people, that the dead were revenged.

The head of the canyon, with its awesome first view of the breaks, brought him to a stop. The north fork of Foster Creek worked its way into the stacked rimrocks, cutting darkly into cliff walls lined with crimson-leafed aspen. The west fork dove from behind the bluff, its wild descent rising up to the golden shivers of the grove under White Buffalo Mountain. And between them, the red rock ledge with the cairn was etched against the sky.

He wondered if Ria were looking down, as if in the straight line of sight, miles as the crows fly, he could hear her if she laughed.

The West Fork coiled from pool to pool, the golden dappling of fallen leaves hiding the clear water sliding underneath. This water passed by the hidden cabin on the journey, passed the cairn, passed the homestead, a continuous line in time from the smooth rocks of the spring where it was born to some distant sea. Sett Foster followed it in his thoughts as the fine bay mare followed it with her sure strong strides.